Gabriel Böhmer

Beetle Days

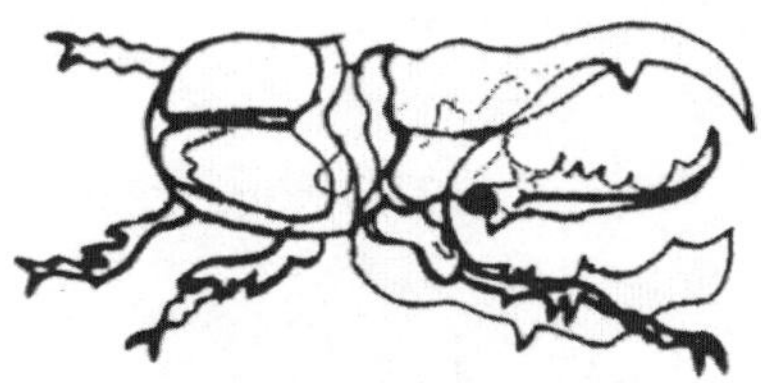

Rational
Vagabund
Books

Rational Vagabund Books
Edinburgh, City of Edinburgh
Scotland, United Kingdom

www.beetledays.com

Book Design: Rational Vagabund

ISBN-10: 0-9896597-1-2
ISBN-13: 978-0-9896597-1-0

To Samantha, the most un-beetley person, and finest adventure companion, anyone could hope for.

PART 1: THE BEETLE MADNESS

Chapter 1

Tim, an unemployed dung beetle, started it all. Usually he just moved shit around to entertain himself. But one day he wandered into a busy department store, climbed onto the tallest shelf, and proclaimed, “A beetle is noble. A beetle has no sense of ownership. Which is why everything belongs to a beetle.”

The baffled faces of shoppers encouraged him to continue.

“As others have a sense of ownership, nothing can belong to anything other than a beetle.”

As soon as he’d made these claims, other beetles inexplicably went about repeating them. It’s important to note that by “a beetle,” each individual beetle was implicating themselves, not their genus.

If they'd considered that every beetle felt this way, it would have caused significant metaphysical debate. But they didn't, because beetles weren't good at listening. People brought this up time and again, and while beetles sometimes pretended to consider the argument, these efforts generally came across as insincere and condescending. Their reasoning was just what it was, and they could not be spoken with sensibly.

There were many different kinds of beetles, and while there were exceptions, they mostly felt the same way. This was astonishing, as their order, coleoptera, contained the most species out of any. But perhaps that just meant it was a normal part of life.

Research into this phenomenon would be conducted for years to come. It was a significant leap in logic that many would never get their heads around. Some remarked on the unusual winter during which most of these beetles had been in eggs. The temperature had beaten record highs and lows on numerous occasions, and increased solar storms had caused ongoing magnetic disturbances. This had resulted in confusion during many animals' migrations. Whales, for instance, kept being spotted in lakes in landlocked countries. Glacier activity had also been curious: some sites had melted at alarming rates, while others had grown. And the weather hadn't become any more normal in the spring.

Then again, the weather was an easy thing to blame. Everyone already did for everything else.

Over time, recitals of the beetle maxim dropped all the a's, eventually declaring:

"Beetle is noble. Beetle has no sense of ownership. Which is why everything belongs to beetle. As others have a sense of ownership, nothing can belong to anything other than beetle."

It was agreed that this removed the problem of attribution, while still giving the impression of speaking about all beetles. Using "beetle" instead of their names had been common already, the latter really only being for legal circumstances, as they unanimously seemed to enjoy the sense of grandeur speaking in the third-beetle gave.

It wasn't long after the beetles' remarks started that John, a man in his late twenties, with dark hair and perpetual stubble, noticed things missing – appropriated by beetles who felt quite strongly that everything belonged to them. He would come home and find chairs or pictures gone. He figured this must have been happening to others as well. The apartment had become decidedly empty in a short period of time, it was really quite amazing what they managed to make off with. Luckily, they didn't care for making coffee and left his old grinder alone. Generally speaking, all John wanted was a good coffee.

Sometimes he could hear the scurrying of little beetle feet as he opened the door, but he rarely caught them stealing. On the handful of occasions that he did, they would offer a barrage of excuses that contradicted themselves. Then they'd speak at great length of a deep sadness in their hearts due to the universe's unfair treatment of beetles. "Beetles," meaning the beetle that was making these statements. Afterwards, they'd insist, with unfounded smugness, on trying to eat from John's dinner plate.

All in all it's better not to catch them, John thought.

This wasn't the year beetles had shown their true nature. That had been the year before. The beetles thought everyone must've forgotten as a result: it was January and a new year, after all. But it had only been a few months, so it was still on people's minds.

***

John had just been on vacation and was on his long way back to the apartment. As the airplane was getting ready to descend, he wondered what would be missing. In that instance, he couldn't recall why he'd bothered with the trip. Not even if it had been good. It all seemed a bit pointless.

He would be in the airport for a few hours, and then board a plane to another country. Despite being an eleven-hour journey apart, the countries shared a language. It wasn't his own.

Where he'd been, was going, or laying-over, really wasn't important. He wasn't really sure what a country was anymore, he realized. None of them were his own. At least, not that he could remember.

As the captain advised the cabin crew to take their seats, John looked out the window. There were beetles on the wing. Five of them.

How are they managing to hold on? he wondered.

John hadn't taken his medication yet. He was saving it for the long flight. It would be his third that day. He'd just been in another place in the country where the language wasn't his own, and he'd come from a different country before that. The turbulence was telling his stomach that something terrible was about to happen. But he'd have to take a lot of medication later, so he didn't want to start now. He knew if he did, he wouldn't be able to walk or speak by the end of the journey. And then he'd feel as if he'd throw up for a day or more. Given the medication's forty-eight-hour half-life, he would already feel numb and slightly happy for a week, and then suddenly very low, with little memory of the past days.

John felt a stinging in the back of his neck. There was a beetle scratching him with one of its claws. He threw it into the aisle. Once it got to its feet, it began complaining.

"Beetle is going to die soon," it said in the third-beetle. "You should be considerate. Beetle is a good beetle." And with that, it ran underneath a seat.

The beetle in question was not going to die soon. That was a beetle-embellishment – something that was quite common. If another beetle had heard it, it would've been possible for it to adopt this falsehood. And once two beetles shared a fabrication, the stories only grew. The root of this mechanism in beetles was unknown. Some scientists estimated that beetle history was only comprised of about twenty percent reliable data. For example, this particular beetle would recall the incident somewhat differently than John would. It would tell of a great oxen stampede on an airplane, which it only survived as a result of its superior genetics.

***

John's country of destination was where he had lived for some years. It wasn't his own. Originally he'd gone there on vacation. He'd ended up staying and now worked at the smallholding and restaurant above which he rented an apartment. It was a little establishment that produced and served food from another country.

Before that, he'd lived in another country that wasn't his either. There he'd worked a professional job but had decided to leave after some time. As his new work paid very little, he'd quickly grown accustomed to no longer having things or money. As a result, the beetles depleting his resources further didn't seem to make a huge difference. It was irritating to look at his bank statements and see withdrawals he hadn't made. But that's just how it was, and nothing could be done after the fact.

When it was time for the long flight, John was already sick to his stomach. He wasn't sure why. He got a sandwich from a vending machine. It was late, and all the restaurants were closed. The food didn't help. All he wanted was a good coffee. He took his medication. As the flight began boarding, walking became a little more difficult. Once his ticket was checked, he wondered why that portable tunnel leading to the aircraft was shaking. But looking at other passengers standing completely still, he realized it wasn't moving at all.

John struggled a little to find his seat, which required reading the ticket, and the area underneath the overhead compartment. As the crew prepared for takeoff, it appeared he had found the correct place. A minor miracle.

Shortly after leaving the ground, there was turbulence, but it was already time for John to take more medication – so he didn't care. It was an older plane, and individual seats didn't have monitors. There was a film playing on the main screen. He tried to pay attention to it but was unable. While he usually avoided plane food, he ate what was served.

As an attendant cleaned up the trays, she asked John, "How was it?" with a friendly smile on her face. There was a beetle sitting on her shoulder. Not the one from the previous flight, a different one. This one was smaller and brown.

"The fries were good, thank you," John replied, trying to be pleasant. His answer prompted a blank look from the attendant.

"You had the pasta." The beetle took an earring without her noticing.

"Of course. Sorry, that's what I meant," John added politely. He wasn't embarrassed. In his state, he was incapable of it. And as the attendant regularly encountered passengers in a similar condition, she focused her attentions elsewhere.

John took more medication. Everything after that became foggy. He mostly slept, deeply and with no dreams. Not how he usually slept. When he woke up, he wasn't in his seat. He wasn't on the plane anymore. It wasn't even the same day.

It was a week later, and he was sitting in his sparse room looking out a dirty window. Everything after getting on the flight seemed like a distant dream. In that moment, he felt completely separate from his history – from all of it, and that was unusual. He wondered where the time had gone. And felt rotten.

He walked down the stairs to the restaurant. Tomas, his employer, was making chicken stock in the kitchen. John asked about the days he was missing, while deciding whether to have wine with his coffee.

Tomas explained that when he'd come to pick him up from the airport, John had refused to get in the car. That he'd wanted to walk around very slowly because he'd felt sick – probably a combination of the plane food and medication, and that after two hours in arrivals, John had been certain it had been only fifteen minutes. When Tomas had convinced him to get in the car, he'd had difficulty putting together words for more than ten seconds at a time. He'd mostly babbled incoherently, and everything had lacked intonation. This had made interpreting the meaning of his words impossible, as one couldn't tell what was serious and what wasn't. The rare occurrence of John being talkative and telling jokes, although funny, had been strange and difficult to understand.

For the rest of the week, he'd seemed content with sitting in one place for hours at a time without saying a word. So Tomas had let him. John's eyes looked old and worried as they often did, but in that moment he'd been thinking of nothing at all.

***

Tomas was a tall and very thin man. He looked as if he never ate, but he ate constantly. His blonde hair was perpetually messy and pointing in all directions. He frequently hunched over when speaking to people to make himself shorter. And he smiled and laughed a little nervously during conversations with strangers. His face told of good and bad times, but his manner preferred to remember only the former.

The country they were in was also not Tomas' own. He'd come with his food from someplace where there was a lot of good cheese, and wine, and produce. At least, so he kept reminding John. Where exactly this was John didn't think important to remember. Neither of them fluently spoke the other one's mother tongue. However, they had an elementary knowledge of a few of the same languages and got by borrowing words from where they could.

Like John, Tomas used to be in a different line of work. He'd been a director at an advertising agency. After a series of illnesses landed him in hospital, a doctor suggested "a slightly more relaxed routine." Always an extremist, Tomas left off the "slightly" and devoted himself to making food – which wasn't actually very relaxing.

He rented two houses on a small piece of land, lived in one, and opened a restaurant out of the other. They were about four meters from each other, which considerably cut down his morning commute. The restaurant was a modest and warm place. Tomas advertised by leaving edible business cards at a friend's farmer's market. They were either biscuits or dried pasta, and all that was on them was a phone number. He only disclosed his address when a reservation was being made. It kept the place quiet. And if he didn't like the sound of someone, they were booked up indefinitely. He'd gained a reputation for eccentricities, but also for good meals.

Diners were served in a square room with a high ceiling, which was made of brick and timber, and painted white like the walls. He hung his daughters' drawings and rotated them as they made new ones. The only permanent wall fixtures were three oversized family photographs that his wife, Sandra, had taken.

It was an old building. The dark, wooden floors were worn, and the furniture looked like it had been collected haphazardly but tastefully. Tomas always littered tables with poetry and books on hypnosis. John liked picking through them, even though they were in a language he didn't fully understand.

On any given night, Tomas used the restaurant to listen to anything from *Paul's Boutique* to *Mule Variations*, usually playing albums from start to finish. But there were nights he just couldn't make up his mind, when one would be lucky to hear a single song all the way through.

Beside the houses was some land where Tomas grew produce. He also raised lambs and chickens. Although not a permanent fixture, over the past two years a big, red bird of prey also spent time there.

Although it was rare, now and then lambs were born with the ability to speak. These were smarter and self-aware. As one could instruct them – somewhat – they worked for a landscaping business that Tomas kept on the side. It wasn't the most efficient or profitable venture. Tomas' speaking sheep had a fairly steady population, which he could just about afford to keep. At the time he had two, Chloé and Jacob, and at most he'd had three. The strange weather had meant that fewer people wanted their gardens cheaply demolished by sheep. It was okay, though. That was just how things went sometimes.

***

When it was time for the sheep to be fed, Tomas gave John the wooden spoon he'd been stirring with and told him to take it easy. Just simmer it. Make sure it doesn't boil. And John obliged. Even though he didn't understand what Tomas had said, it didn't matter. He knew how to make stock.

Tomas went outside, whistling intermittently, and first checked on the chickens. He put their eggs in a basket and then grabbed two buckets of feed from the shed. He fed the mute sheep, at which he always made clicking sounds, and then walked over to the others with their feed.

"Good morning, Jacob. Good morning, Chloé," Tomas said.

"Good morning, Tomas," Chloé replied, and then Jacob. Tomas looked out at the small field. Both sheep stopped trying to graze on the underdeveloped grass in the pen, and joined him.

"Nice day, no? It's so clear. You can see really far," Tomas said. Beyond the property, the view was mixed. Some of the landscape was made up of ugly factories with big smoke stacks, and there were the train tracks quite close by. But other parts were nice, with fields and farmland.

"Yes, but to see far is strange. How can an enclosure be so big, Tomas?" Jacob asked in his calm and innocent way.

Tomas stopped whistling and thought for a minute. "Well, not everything is an enclosure."

Chloé's ears twitched, and she looked up at Tomas with a scrunched brow. "What do you mean?" she asked.

Tomas looked at her. When he opened his mouth to reply, he realized he didn't know how. He looked back out and was now confused himself. "I guess it's difficult to explain. But, there's a lot of land outside this enclosure."

"And this land never ends?" Chloé asked, her eyes widened in amazement.

"Oh no, it ends. Where it meets the ocean."

"What's the ocean, Tomas?" Jacob asked, as he squinted his eyes. "I can't see it."

"It's too far to see. The ocean is water."

"So the ocean is a fence made of water, and land is a really big enclosure," Chloé said. Tomas smiled as he filled their trough.

"Yes, Chloé, I guess that's true." She was happy that she understood, while Jacob now felt uncomfortable and thought there were many more questions.

"So if we're in an even bigger enclosure, does that mean there are people that can't speak? Ones that other animals eat?" he asked.

"There are people who can't speak, but mostly no one eats them. A wolf might, if he had the chance. But a wolf might eat any person if he had the chance."

"But people don't get eaten because even people without words have guns?" Jacob asked, remembering the terrible sound the things made. And how the sound had killed animals in the past.

Tomas considered but then simply said, "Yes."

"Tomas, if this land is a bigger enclosure, why do the people in that big house make it dirty with smoke?" Chloé asked. "The grass and air around it must be bad."

Tomas frowned as he looked at the factory and traced its smoke with his eyes high up into the clouds. *It'd be impossible to eat Chloé*, he thought. "I don't know, Chloé. I don't." Both sheep were shocked.

Jacob now became increasingly worried and said, "Tomas, are you sick?"

"No. Why do you ask?"

"Because you know everything… You must've had some bad grass," he concluded.

Tomas laughed. "Yes, I think you're right."

The sheep began eating. After hearing him laugh, they felt satisfied that once the grass went through his system, Tomas would know everything again.

***

International regulations did not recognize speaking animals as distinct from mute ones, but Tomas felt strongly that eating them was immoral.

Extensive research had concluded that the difference between speaking and mute animals was negligible. However, it's of note that discount supermarket chains were the sole sponsors of the investigation. Critics of the study pointed out that they had a vested interest. Selling every animal kept margins as high as possible. Tomas called this "evil economics."

Academics tried using news organizations to expose the flaws behind the investigation. But in the end, the study's apt title, "Let Us Eat Everything Except People, For Now," distracted the public from the real topic, which may or may not have been its intended purpose. And recently people discussed the beetle problem more than anything else. So the talking animals agenda drifted into the background.

Tomas continued being passionate about giving his animals a nice life. When cooking, he'd sometimes turn to John and say, "If someone gave me the option of having the best life imaginable, why should I object to being eaten?"

Tomas generally didn't buy lambs that someone else might. He preferred those that'd been rejected, or whose mother had died, which he then purchased for close to nothing from his neighbor and landlord Martín. Martín was a sheep farmer who raised valais blacknose: fluffy white animals with black feet and faces. They were from a different country and a long way from home. Martín did not have the time to raise orphans. If no one wanted them, he'd put them down, so Tomas always bought them. And he was very fond of them. John liked them too, because he remembered the breed from his childhood.

Tomas hand-raised his lambs. It was very time-consuming and difficult. He'd give them names, and pet them, and chat with them, when he knew full well he shouldn't.

The day after picking John up, Tomas had to drive to the abattoir. He could have used John's help, but John didn't seem to be quite there, he simply stared into the distance for long periods of time. Tomas got two of the mute ones in the truck by persuading them with food. It was the same beat-up old thing from the sixties that he always borrowed off Martín. Somehow, his mechanics kept managing to bring it back to life. It produced an incredible amount of black exhaust, but no one wanted to get rid of it. Tomas ran his steady hands along the textured outside and inspected the new colors that'd shown up on the hood. At some point it'd been red. Tomas liked how the truck kept changing, and a smile appeared on his face as he forgot about the sheep for a few seconds.

Inside the truck, it was the same as always, his fingers felt numb, and his arms shook as he turned the keys in the ignition, and he felt sick.

Tomas wasn't allowed to kill the lambs on his property. If he had been, he would have. But then he wouldn't have been able to sell the meat at the restaurant. He got in the car and, after some time on the dirt path, pulled onto the two-lane road he'd take all the way. There were accidents there all the time, caused by wild horses and people's dogs. The dogs usually died. One could see a collared carcass every few hundred meters in some spots. Tomas stopped focusing on the road. He could see the two animals through the rearview mirror. He spent more time looking at them than at where he was going. He knew where he was going. And if an animal wandered into the road, he wouldn't have time to stop anyway.

Tomas watched his animals' ears against the moving landscape and thought to himself:

They've had a nice life. And this is what sheep are for. Not to take home, and curl up with, and have at the dinner table. They're for on the dinner table. This is what they're for... right? Is it? Really? If I hadn't raised them, then they wouldn't have had a life at all. They're not pets. And if I just start keeping them, then we can only keep a few. Hell, I'm already doing that with the talking ones. And that would mean no longer buying any new ones. No new ones to have a nice life. And then people will just get their meat from the other bastards, where there is never a nice life.

And we'll make good use of the meat. Every part. As much as possible. They'll be damned delicious. It'll be delicious. What more could be expected than that? And by serving such nice meat, more people will want it. And this will make more bastard farmers give their bastard animals a nicer life. A really nice life. And bastard people will be able to buy less meat if they only buy the nice, expensive meat. And this will lower the bastards' intensive breeding and bad conditions. And so on and so bastard forth. I think.

He repeated iterations of these thoughts throughout the car ride to the slaughterhouse. He witnessed the deed. And when the deed was done, it was as always: his spirits were lifted by the fine product, in spite of how he felt about it all.

He drove back and hung the meat in the cold box to age. He looked at *it* proudly. There was no more *them*. After a few glasses of wine that evening, he began talking of the lamb and its quality. Sandra had heard this speech a few times and went to bed immediately. A recently appointed waiter got stuck listening for a number of hours. He was too new and polite to excuse himself. He also happened to be a vegetarian, and didn't particularly agree with Tomas' views.

Because of this life, Tomas had become more aware about what he consumed, and what died because of him. No matter how convenient, mass production had lost its appeal.

"Meat, fish, eggs, vegetables – anything has to come from the right place. Otherwise they're just pretending to be those things," Tomas would tell John. Everyone who worked at the restaurant ate the little meat they could vouch for, a lot of produce from the garden, and fish from some guy who caught them by hook and line. It was all that was available to them. The unusual weather had led to modest takings, but they had all they needed. If they'd had to buy everything, it would've been difficult to keep things running.

Tomas hadn't minded beetles until their madness. If anything, he'd found them quite useful. There'd been plenty of dung-spinning beetles who seemed downright decent. They used to recycle the nutrients in the soil, doing marvels for its structure, and kept the area hygienic for the animals. But when the whole revolt thing began, they were suddenly too good for their old jobs. They wanted to live in houses, and sleep in their beds, and eat in the dining room for free. No more work, ever. And despite their small size, beetles insisted on sitting on one chair each. He had to eject them from the restaurant on a regular basis now, and they always made a big fuss about it. This was embarrassing, but clients had become used to seeing that sort of thing. It was the way of things everywhere. Tomas had a sense of ownership, so it only made sense for beetles to claim what was his as theirs. Tomas began formulating theories about how supermarket chains had caused all this, and that it was simply a way of diverting attention from the speaking animals issue.

Chapter 2

The summer wasn't too hot that year, and the general cycle of things seemed to be back in order. Trees, and flowers, and fruits, and vegetables were growing as they were supposed to. Everyone agreed that things were very pleasant – besides the beetles, of course. But there was nothing that could be done. One had to take things a day at a time: ignore the beetles when possible, and deal with them when one had to.

John and Tomas had spent most their lives in places where this time of year was winter. But they were in the southern hemisphere now, and the seasons were the opposite. They'd both been there a while, and John had begun thinking of summer as December onwards, but there was still something strange and special about it. Tomas could never make the switch. At times they could've done with seeing a snowy landscape, but generally feeling warm in December felt exciting. Friends in the northern hemisphere continued to be confused. They couldn't understand how it could be summer when it was winter.

***

Tomas swore that where he was from, lambs were only born in spring. But Martín seemed to get new ones at random, and a few had been born recently. Tomas was making red wine butter with shallots when the phone rang. A wolf got a mother. So it went sometimes. The lamb was young and had to be fed several times a day and at night.

Tomas walked over to his landlord's. It was a proper farm, but there was less space per animal. One of the farm workers pointed at the little lamb. He looked like a strange statue, one that just needlessly pointed at things.

Tomas petted the lamb's head and scratched behind her ear. She spoke a bit in the language that was her own. He picked her up and walked back to the smallholding. He named her Emily. He didn't think she'd develop speech, but for reasons he couldn't explain he put her in Jacob and Chloé's pen. She timidly sat down in a corner, away from the others. Tomas clicked his tongue and snapped his fingers at her, but she wasn't interested. She didn't respond to anything of the sort, even to things mute ones usually would.

Over the next few days, he fed Emily by hand as much as she'd eat. But she didn't grow. She stayed small and pretty-looking. After two weeks, Tomas became concerned and called the local vet. For some reason, no one could ever remember his name. He was a gangly man in his fifties with a rather nervous and depressed disposition. His balding head and wrinkled face depicted a much older man. Although an excellent diagnostician, he hated breaking bad news. This led to his gaining a reputation of not being cut out for the job. He was known to mope around local bars but wasn't much of a drinking man. Instead, he'd just sit in front of a glass for hours and would feel inebriated after a pint of beer and lemonade. In this state he took people's greetings to mean they harbored bad thoughts about him.

After various medical exams, the vet concluded that there was nothing wrong with Emily. He was overjoyed. Upon first seeing her, he was sure she'd have to be put down. Everything had to be put down. Always. But for once, that wasn't the case. It seemed that she would simply be a lamb forever. Always young. Tomas wasn't sure if such a lamb could be eaten and was confused as to what he was going to do with her. The ambiguity of Emily's purpose brought the vet right back down. He left the smallholding the same way he left everywhere else: more depressed than when he'd gotten there.

In the following weeks, Emily became increasingly comfortable in her new home. One day, when Tomas came to the pen and asked, "How are you this morning, Emily?" the little lamb finally looked up at him.

"Who's Emily? Is it me? My mother called me by a different name. Although it's difficult to remember now. It was so long ago. At least it is for me," she said. Tomas dropped the bucket of food he was carrying. Hearing a lamb speak for the first time was always a surprise, no matter how many times it happened.

"What did your mother call you?" he asked inquisitively after processing what'd occurred.

"Baa."

Tomas smiled. Emily's mother hadn't been a talking sheep. "That's not your name, that's just the sound sheep make," he told her.

Emily tilted her head to the side, which inadvertently caused the bell around her neck to ring. She was confused. She made all sorts of sounds, after all. But in what was left of her memories, her mother did repeat a very limited range of noises. *What could that mean?* she wondered.

"You can call me Emily, if you like. I guess you don't understand the language that is our own. But I'm going to keep calling myself Baa, if that's alright," she said, glad to have come up with a compromise.

"That's just fine," Tomas said.

Emily became very social. She was curious about all the animals and quickly became friends with Jacob and Chloé. And although the cats, Lucy and Socks, didn't say much, they did enjoy sleeping near her in the hay every now and then. Emily also insisted on talking with the mute sheep and chickens, and would never admit that their conversational skills were comparatively limited. Anyway, sometimes it was nice to speak to someone who just listened.

Tomas watched her be friendly with a mute lamb from the kitchen. Their pens weren't far apart, and they could easily hear and see each other. There was something macabre about it, but right then Tomas was more fascinated than anything else. He opened the window so he could overhear the conversation, while he prepared some of the more time-intensive dishes for the evening service.

"Nice day, isn't it?" Emily said to the mute lamb.

"Baa," it replied.

"Have you been here long?"

"Baa."

“I got here not that long ago. Do you like the food?”

“Baa.” Chloé and Jacob stopped eating and squinted at Emily with curiosity. To them, all this incessant baaing seemed like ridiculous gibberish.

“You understand them,” Chloé said, her voice quivering.

“Not a word,” Emily replied nonchalantly.

Tomas closed the window and was unable to contain a smile while going about his work. He told people of that conversation throughout the night. By the time the last table had left, John had heard it a few too many times and couldn’t help feeling that there was actually something sad about it. Eventually Tomas could see that John needed a break and told him to have a beer outside. Being alone felt nice after a long day. He’d brought one of Tomas’ books on hypnosis and tried to read. His dark hair fell into his eyes, and he threatened it, insisting it would be shaved off for annoying him. Then he saw Beetle walking up the path to the restaurant.

Beetle was a beetle that John was very familiar with. He showed up frequently and seemed to enjoy annoying John to no end. Beetle was quite an ordinary-looking thing. One could rightly say that his opinions and behavior were the epitome of beetle thought. Why he'd come to keep bugging John was beyond him. But that's just how it was. John had seen Beetle taking things from his apartment, but Beetle always denied his crimes wholeheartedly. Even when caught beetle-handed.

Apparently it was time for one of their fun little chats. Sometimes John just wanted to step on Beetle. As Beetle crawled onto an outdoor table, John looked inside, hoping that Sandra might join him for a glass of wine like she sometimes did. Beetle preferred to irritate John in private, and if she came outside, he usually left.

"Beetle is three-hundred million years old," Beetle said in the third-beetle. "John, what are you? Two-hundred thousand?" Something about beetle speech was always painful to listen to. It wasn't quite the right pitch. As if it were too high and too low at the same time. And it wavered constantly, like an old radio that'd been dropped too many times.

"That's a lot of years. You're very old. I'm twenty-nine."

"Twenty-nine. That's ridiculous! You don't know anything," Beetle said as a matter of fact.

"Is that so?" John took a big gulp of beer and tried to think of something to which he could change the topic. "Hey, I was just wondering, if perhaps you've been... borrowing stuff from my place again?" John was still hoping to get some of his things back. He was just trying to figure out what the price would be.

"I never have! How dare you say that? Beetle doesn't need your crappy things. Beetle has no sense of ownership. Bet you feel bad now for ever mentioning it."

"That doesn't mean you haven't taken anything."

"Beetle could get them back for you. Beetle is extremely well connected. It will be a great inconvenience to Beetle, but Beetle could look into it, since you're begging. You'd really owe Beetle a big one, though."

This was a road John didn't want to go down. "Don't worry about it. I don't need it. As you said, just crap."

"No, no. You already asked. So Beetle will do you this favor. Just this once." Beetle couldn't suppress a smile appearing on his face. He figured John wasn't bright enough to notice, anyway. And if he were, he wouldn't know why it was there.

"No, thanks. Nice night, eh?" John stared at the stars, and their beauty gave him a quiet comfort. He couldn't rationalize why, but that was the effect the inconceivably giant and distant bodies had on him.

"Oh, now you change your mind, when Beetle has already wasted so much time on preparations and made himself look like a fool for you. Make up your brain, you idiot!" Beetle frowned at John, and John simply gazed skywards. Neither of them said anything. John tried to name the constellations he saw, and began breathing more easily. He'd known how to identify them when he'd been a boy, but now he couldn't remember any of it.

Finally, some silence, John thought.

But it was short-lived, and Beetle quickly began again. "A great beetle war is coming," he said very seriously.

"Is that so? Seems to be the word around." John's voice was flat, as if he were reading the chemical makeup of a bar of soap.

"Guess who will be beetle king," Beetle said, sticking his nose in the air now and smiling again.

"I don't know." John couldn't get himself to look at Beetle. He knew what he wanted him to say.

"Beetle will be king of beetles. All the other beetles are pleading with Beetle." This was a falsehood. Not a single beetle had asked Beetle to be king. "Beetle wasn't interested really. Beetle has so many important things to do with his intellect. But it's true that there is no one as well-suited and qualified as Beetle." Beetle gave a big sigh. "Guess somebody has to do it. Might as well be the best." Beetle's chivalry caused

John to laugh. Beetle visibly took great offence and grimaced. "It's a great honor! What are you laughing at, you insignificant, arrogant little shit? You have a tremendously inflated sense of self-worth. And no one's ever going to make you a king if you keep that up!" If there was something beetles couldn't stand, it was being laughed at. There was a long pause between the two. John was hoping Beetle would just leave now. But Beetle just sat there, fuming and eyeing him.

Sandra finally came out with a glass of wine and a coffee for John. Good coffee happened to be her specialty. John looked back to where Beetle was sitting and was pleasantly surprised to see that he was already gone.

After drinking the coffee, John went inside to help clean up the kitchen. It was late, and the cats wanted to be fed. They always tried to get at people's leftovers, but John didn't think this scavenging was good manners. Sandra and Tomas couldn't help themselves, though, and gave the cats scraps when John wasn't looking.

They were a breed of forest cat, from a cold country in the north and far away. Lucy was mostly white on her face, stomach, and legs, and had a light gray, tabby back, tail, and ears. Socks was almost entirely a deep, fiery orange, except for a white patch on his chest and his white feet. They each had two coats of fur and looked wild and pleasant at the same time. They were siblings. And their great-great-great-ancestors came over with their owners. Of course, neither of them knew anything of this. Nor was it important nor interesting to them.

They were both nice cats and enjoyed hunting, keeping the place free of mice and any other pests. Although Lucy was smaller than her brother, she was the leader and did most the talking. Being a cat, however, she was naturally reserved with her words and felt that actions spoke a fair amount louder. While kind and sweet to John and the others, the two were vicious to vermin and enjoyed killing in rather unsympathetic ways. A favorite game of theirs was to catch mice but not harm them. And then take turns repeatedly and violently throwing them against walls.

Lucy and Socks were technically Tomas' cats, but John had been there since they'd come from a dairy farm up the road. He was also the only one who slept in the same house as them. So while he was strict with them, they'd still taken to him the most.

***

John was trying to lead a simple life, filled with the things he enjoyed. But sometimes, especially at night, his mind was clouded. He couldn't think straight. When he tried to sleep, he couldn't stop his brain from jumping from thought to thought. And then there was the late train around two fifteen that would wake him if he happened to be asleep. But most troubling was that, when the sun set, his thoughts became odd and foreign.

That night was the same as always. When he finally drifted into unconsciousness, he had vivid dreams. But he had no idea where the images came from – as if, when his brain finally turned the lights off, it was reading from a book with which John was unfamiliar. Not the plot, the setting, or the characters. And it always had something to do with the thoughts and experiences of some beetle named Jolobo. And these dreams tended to weave through strange monologues, in which the words, "The eyes of the man are never satisfied," were frequently repeated.

There was, however, one thing that John recognized from his dreams: a constant tapping. This led to the suspicion that all of it had something to do with a death watch beetle. His name was Abaddon, and he lived in the rafters above John's bed. He spoke too quietly for people to understand him when they were awake, so John didn't actually know his name. He was a dark brown beetle with light flecks on his back. John wasn't sure if that was his natural coloring or sawdust from when he ate the house's wood. He looked old and had a deep, kind voice. And as far as John could tell, he always behaved pleasantly, which was why he'd never thought to evict him.

The only annoying thing about Abaddon was his constant tapping in the summer. But John figured that at his age a peculiarity or two was to be expected. If he'd known anything about death watch beetles, he'd have realized that Abaddon's tapping had nothing to do with age. He was simply trying to impress potential dates with his talents as a percussionist. On the other hand, if one were to listen to Abaddon's words, it would be clear that he was a pest of the highest order.

John lay in bed, and Abaddon quietly began his chatter. Not loud enough for John to register the words, but loud enough for them to echo in his dreams.

"Have fear in the wake of the morning." Tap, tap, tap.

"Even the honeycombs in your life will taste bitter." Tap, tap.

"You have wasted the sands of the hourglass." Tap, tap, tap.

"And you should be ashamed." Tap.

"And you will not eat from the fig tree." Tap.

"As you did not guard it." Tap, tap, tap.

"You will die pitiful and in pain, when the sun begins its slumber." Tap, tap.

"Because a great meteor is coming." Tap, tap.

"And all of this hurts Abaddon, but he fears it is true, because he can see the future... You were born of a wicked blood." Tap, tap, tap.

"And you bear ugliness in your soul and upon your flesh." Tap.

"And foreseeable evil will punish you." Tap.

"And you are at fault for the suffering of your fellow creatures." Tap, tap, tap.

"And you'll be a fool forever." Tap, tap.

"But Abaddon will continue to grind you."

It was during one of Abaddon's intermissions that John fell asleep. Abaddon then said, "The eyes of the man are never satisfied," and continued with what sounded like deep, friendly rumbling.

Lucy and Socks hated Abaddon. They hated all beetles, but him in particular. His rumbling infuriated them. Not only was their hearing good enough to understand every word he was saying, but they also detested the idea that, to others, Abaddon sounded like he was purring.

They'd tried telling John what Abaddon said, but the subject made them so angry that they could only explain themselves in cat, and John didn't understand cat. On this day, as on many others, they attempted to climb the beams of the house to get at him. As far as they were concerned, any imposter that used purring for the sake of evil was as good as dead.

John was woken by their shouting and climbing. Socks yelled at Abaddon in cat, which sounded as if he were trying to imitate a bird. Lucy didn't see the point in this, and instead tried giving the beetle a false sense of security in human.

"Let's be friends. Come here," she said in a soothing tone, over and again, as she dug her sharp claws into the wood and crawled ever closer.

Although confused at first, John was glad to have been released from a strange dream. He didn't understand what they were up to but found their antics amusing. To save them from getting hurt, he stopped them before they got too high. They were disappointed. They thought that it may have been Abaddon's last day. But now John was putting them outside the bedroom and closing the door. He lay back down on the bed and began the familiar sequence of trying to sleep once more.

John had not taken his medication. He knew if he did, he'd sleep right away, but it would not be a restful sleep. It would just be darkness. And then he would wake the next day and feel as if he hadn't slept.

Although Socks frantically patted the door with his paws, both cats knew John wouldn't let them in. Lucy tried reasoning with him, but all that came out was, "Let us in! The meooow mowww meeeow!"

They sat, powerless and upset, as they heard Abaddon say once more, "The eyes of the man are never satisfied." And with that John fell into a strange slumber.

He could see through the eyes of the beetle Jolobo. He walked in a wasteland. But he also saw him from the outside. As if he were Jolobo, and watching him, at the same time. There was yellow and red sand everywhere, and dunes in the distance. Their round edges looked soft and shimmered in the heat, but their texture was as crude and hard as everything else. Jolobo wasn't thinking just then. He was only walking. From the cloudless sky beat a hard and vengeful sun. Jolobo's exoskeleton was peeling from the constant exposure.

I am hungry and thirsty, Jolobo thought. It'd been a long time since his last meal. He should've been dead. If he'd stopped to think about it, he would've wished he were. But mostly, Jolobo did not think. He simply was. Often it seemed that he was the sole inhabitant of this world. But he did not consider or deliberate on this either. *Thirsty, and also hungry*, he reminded himself.

He was beautiful. His head resembled the skull of some ancient animal. His horns looked like jaws and jagged teeth, like the remains of some prehistoric wolf. His body shimmered a deep, pleasing black, and on his back were striking gold speckles.

Jolobo moved his feet and slipped in the sand. Constantly scraping forward. More of the same. It was the only thing that was real, and there was no need for anything else. He required no encouragement in what appeared to be pointless. How Jolobo came to be or how he arrived at this place was unimportant, and also forgotten.

Jolobo very suddenly found himself in front of a dead tree. It looked as if it had fallen over a long time ago, and its trunk and branches now hugged the ground. It was big, and dull, and silver, and peeling. It'd been alive for many years. But the land around it gave no indication that something like this could inhabit this tundra.

Maybe there is food, Jolobo considered as he crawled onto a branch. His claws stopped sweeping sand and begun to tick and tap on the new surface. Wind came and went, and with it the ground – tiny rocks and dust spinning effortlessly in the air, slowly filling the branch's deep cracks. Jolobo made it onto the trunk of the tree. He stopped walking as the wind picked up and threatened to blow him off.

Brace, he thought to himself. He lowered his body close to the wood. One of the tree's weaker branches snapped in the wind. It gave a big crack that could be felt. It fell quickly and blew off across the ground. Soon it wasn't even visible anymore. The sand was now beginning to fill the cracks in the beetle's body, penetrating the little spaces between his exoskeleton. The wind stopped. Jolobo continued walking, and the sand slowly rolled off him. It also fell off the gray tree, making a fantastic and big sound, like the ocean retreating. And the tree was becoming part of the sand. As the elements wore it down, it had no alternative but to break off, little by little. Flaking gray pieces mixing with the red and yellow. Baking in the sun. Changing to resemble the source of its end.

Jolobo put his front left claw against the tree and pushed off. Just another step. But right as he was about to advance, he slipped, and his claw went into a crack. One that seemed to exist for the appendage. And now that it had found him, it wouldn't let him go. He pulled at his leg, but it would not come out. Jolobo walked in a circle around his foot and then backwards, tracing his path.

Stuck, Jolobo thought. He pulled once more, but the tree would not release him. A strong wind came, and with it, more sand. Jolobo thought, *Brace again*, and hunkered down to receive nature. He dug his claws into the dry wood with all his might. But after some time, his strength began to give, and his body shook and tapped against the tree.

A particularly large gust lifted Jolobo off the earth, but he wasn't sent flying high up in the air. Instead he violently fluttered just above the tree, his stuck claw keeping him anchored. This thrashing was wearing on his front-left joint. But just as he felt his exoskeleton being pulled apart, the wind died down. He floated no more.

It took him a second to get his legs in the right order, and then Jolobo tried walking again. He was determined to be no longer attached to the tree and risk being caught by the wind again. He could fly of course, but he knew that in these conditions it would be pointless. He wasn't a particularly good flier, because of his size. He used his entire body to pull at the claw once more, and finally he was free. But not without a cost. His leg was still in the tree. He'd pulled so hard that it'd been ripped clear off his body.

As Jolobo limped along, he considered his legs. *Five*, he thought and felt that this wasn't quite right. He looked back at where he'd come from and saw his leg, standing up and curved, like a serpent about to attack. Jolobo looked at where it should've been and then limped back to his leg. He inspected it.

It is foreign now, and I am still the same, he thought, before turning around and continuing onwards. With each step, he grew more accustomed to five legs. And after a few minutes, the rest of his limbs seamlessly divided the workload of the old front-left leg.

Outside John's mind, and in his bedroom, Abaddon said, "The eyes of the man are never satisfied."

Chapter 3

"What is happy?" Emily asked one morning when getting a bath. "Is it stretching your face and making the same noise again and again?"

"Happy isn't an action or a behavior," Tomas answered as he shampooed her head. "It's a feeling that you hope you get from surrounding yourself with things you love."

"Like presents?"

"It's not usually things. It's friends, and work, and how you live, and how you treat each other, and how happy they are." One of the wait staff came outside, and took a picture of the mute sheep, and then collected some eggs. She smiled at Tomas and took a picture of him and Emily before going back in.

"So to be happy, your friends need to be happy. And your friends need you to be happy for them to be happy. It all sounds very complicated," Emily said.

"It is. When you're little, it's easier sometimes."

"Because your friends are smaller?" The chickens were clucking happily while searching for food. *They're smaller and they seem less complicated,* Emily thought.

"No… You can have big friends. It's because you haven't learned to be unhappy yet. It's a very difficult thing to unlearn, and everyone learns it. Some earlier than others, but eventually everyone does."

"What do you do then?"

"You can either accept that sometimes you'll be happy, and sometimes you won't, or you can decide not to really feel either anymore. A lot of people choose not to feel either. It's easier." Emily saw Lucy running and jumping against the restaurant, over and again. Tomas' watch was reflecting the sunlight onto the wall, and as he moved his hand the spot of light bobbed up and down. Lucy was determined to kill it.

"Lucy the cat is always happy." Lucy crouched down in the grass. She got very low to the ground, and even flattened her ears. As she became more excited by the light, her tail slowly rose up, and rhythmically moved from left to right.

"She's not always happy. She's just one of those rare creatures that always make themselves appear happy. If only for the sake of those around her. She's very special. It takes a lot of effort, and not many can do it. When she's sad, it's much worse, because she doesn't let anyone see." Tomas got some water and washed the soap off Emily. Now his watch was behind the lamb, and no longer cast a light on the restaurant. Lucy looked for the light, but couldn't find it, and so she began vigorously cleaning her right back paw instead.

"The vet is always sad, but he doesn't seem to need a lot of effort for that," Emily said.

Tomas laughed and shook his head. "I don't think he can help himself. He often has to tell people bad news."

"Lucy would still behave happy, if she was the vet." Emily was completely washed, and she shook herself to get some of the water out of her fur. Tomas sat on a patch of grass, and began picking at the weeds around him.

"Yes, I think you're right."

"Is this happy, Tomas?"

"What do you mean?"

"This place. It's happier and sadder than Martín's. So I don't know if it's happy or sad."

"What do you think?"

"I think Martín's wasn't either. And that this is happy, but with sad bits," Emily said, and Tomas thought she was the smartest sheep he'd ever met. Chloé and Jacob could make observations, but they never spoke the way she did. "And because Martín's farm couldn't be either, it made it a bit sad all the time," she added.

"That sounds right. This place is both, I guess," Tomas confirmed, but he could see Emily was confused. "I think something that can be really happy, can only do so by also being really sad sometimes." The mute sheep were shouting at a crow, and the crow shouted back. *Perhaps it's communication,* Tomas thought.

"Are you sad?" Emily asked, tilting her head to the side.

"Most of the time I'm not. Sometimes I am." Without his smile, Tomas' face suddenly looked its age. "Everyone is."

Emily looked out into the distance. "Sadness has something to do with talking," she said. "But it's good." Tomas took a towel hanging from the fence and began drying the lamb.

"Is it?"

"Yeah. It's better than not being able to." A drunk ladybird flew by Emily's nose, causing her to sneeze, which put the ladybird slightly off course. After regaining its composure it flew along, while cursing the world for such unfair treatment.

Just then, Tomas could hear the phone beginning to ring again. It'd been going on all day. He walked to the restaurant, but John had already picked it up. The last few times Tomas had got it, it'd also been for John. And the phone in John's apartment had been ringing non-stop as well.

"Is this John?" Someone said on the other end of the line.

"Yes."

"This is the police calling, John. We need you to come in, so we can arrest you forever."

"Is that so?" After hearing more than two words, it was easy to guess that he was speaking to a beetle. Their strange voices always gave them away. Recently, it had always been a beetle. They asked stupid questions and made ridiculous statements to amuse themselves. Occasionally one could hear snickering on the other end of the line. It was other beetles listening in and laughing at the absurdity of the whole thing.

"Yeah, you're getting locked up, and we're throwing away the key. You'll be inside for a long time."

"What crimes do I stand accused of?" There was a prolonged pause.

"Having… stupid… hair." Giggling could be heard. "And not paying your… eh… alive tax."

"I had no idea there was an alive tax."

"Yeah, of course. You're alive, aren't you? There's a tax on that. But maybe we can figure something out. Just leave all your money and things outside the house, and we'll come pick it up. We can maybe get you a reduced sentence that way." Now there was chuckling and shushing.

"That's very nice of you." John's voice was calm and without intonation.

"But if you don't do something about that stupid hair, you're still going away for life. At the very least!" With that, the beetles couldn't contain themselves any longer. Loud roars of laughter could be heard.

John calmly hung up. He didn't want Tomas to be able to guess that it was another one of the calls. John had spent the morning trying to complete his tasks and getting to the phone first. It was a nuisance, and he had no idea why he was being targeted.

John had unplugged the phone in his apartment. He couldn't do the same in the restaurant, though. They needed it in case someone wanted to make a reservation. John and Tomas would've bickered about all this if they'd only been able to competently speak the same language. As they couldn't, each of them simply went about their tasks, loudly and deliberately.

When lunchtime came around, John just wanted some peace and quiet. He walked outside and strolled toward the end of the property. When he got to the old, grey, and cracking bench at the edge of their field, he took a notebook and pen from his back pocket.

John was writing down the morning's events. At the end of a week, it was difficult for him to remember what'd happened. And he didn't like it. He felt comforted by recording things as they occurred and being able to remind himself of what had taken place.

He'd only just sat down and was about to begin when he became aware of a presence. John looked around the bench. He couldn't see anyone. When he looked back down at his book, Beetle was sitting on it and looking up at him.

"John, you're not taking your medication?" Beetle asked in his relaxed yet grating voice.

"You can see I haven't. Don't need it," John replied hurriedly trying to stop his words from coming out with the annoyance he felt. He hated Beetle's questions, especially when they were poorly disguised statements.

"You should."

"Why is that?" John was doing his best to be pleasant, but he was having a hard time and spoke through clenched teeth.

"Because it's all going to get much worse, and you know how you get," Beetle said condescendingly.

"I'm perfectly fine."

"You're not. You only think you are, because you haven't grasped the danger. You just aren't smart enough, if we're honest with each other."

"Then let's not be honest with each other. Have you been calling the house?"

"Beetle has better things to do, don't be ridiculous. Beetle can solve the problem for you though," he said in the third-beetle.

“Not interested. Leave me alone.” Beetle walked around, bored, looking for something to entertain himself with. Then he realized he was standing on John’s open notebook.

“What’s this you’re writing, John? Your diary? That’s pathetic. Only little girls do that. Beetle will read it and tell you it’s bad,” Beetle insisted, his eyes already intently scanning the words.

“No you won’t. Get lost.” John brushed Beetle onto the floor and closed the book. He decided writing would have to wait and instead began eating a sandwich he’d brought.

“Tomas poisoned your food. He’s trying to kill you.” John stopped for a moment, but then replayed the words in his head and rolled his eyes at himself.

“No, he didn’t. Don’t be fucking absurd.”

“He did, beetle saw him,” he insisted.

“No, you didn’t. I made this. Even the bread.” There was a pause.

“You should let Beetle eat it.”

“No. Go away.” Beetle began laughing. He could see John was irritated.

"John, you're embarrassing yourself. Trust Beetle. Take your medication. It's what's best for you," he said, earnestly pitying John in that moment, and he let out an emphasized sigh. But then a smile quickly crawled across Beetle's face.

"Trust you? You know what I think of your ideas?" John considered his next words.

"Oh, what's that? Please, do tell," Beetle said mockingly.

Lucy ran over to see who John was talking to. She could hear that he was annoyed, even all the way from the house. Socks could too, but preferred to hide underneath the stairs when John was irritated. John looked at Lucy and then back to Beetle. But he was already gone.

Lucy's face was worried, her eyes were wide open and sad, and her ears drooped down on either side, and her tail was on the ground. While she rarely used words, she was very expressive. John pet her head, and that seemed to cheer her up a little bit. She became even happier when a ladybird – or "ladybug," or "god's cow" – flew by. Something to chase. Not kill, since she liked them, just play with. Lucy's tail and ears cheerfully went up as she began hopping after it. The ladybird flew desperately for its life.

Ladybirds were technically beetles, but they felt quite different than the rest of their order. Really, they had enough problems as it was without cats chasing them.

Although people and animals were unaware of it, ladybirds had become rather miserable as a species, and they spent a lot of time considering the meaning of their existence and that of the world around them. In that state, many ladybirds had begun to create some awful music and paintings. Very whiny stuff, that only another beetle prone to moaning about everything could enjoy. It would've been comedic, if it hadn't been so sad. Sad that they felt this was of any merit.

It had become all the rage, though. Every second ladybird said they were a writer, or a painter, or something else. They would rarely practice their disciplines, but when they did, it was without an iota of skill or talent. There were a few who weren't too bad, but any good work always ended up being abused in one way or another.

Among the artistically inclined, there was a beetle called Frank. The morning Emily was born, the ladybird council officially declared that he wrote the best free verses around. He was a most shiny and colorful beetle and was also considered quite handsome. Although lacking in life experience, Frank wrote passionately and eloquently about just that. And his words resonated with many a beetle, not just ladybirds.

They were written in beetle, however, so his works were never to be enjoyed by any other order. He was known to make a fool of himself after chewing on wine grapes, although this was largely overlooked, as his verses were profound statements about the meaning of the beetle condition. Some called him an absurdist, others – an existentialist. A few were convinced that he was in fact a nihilist. In reality, beetles were not familiar enough with any of these doctrines to be making such statements. Although it is difficult to imagine, those who judged and discussed the others' art tended to be even more pretentious than the creators themselves.

One particularly well-regarded poem of Frank's was "Of Life and Ownership." Ladybirds took to quoting one or two lines of it to show others that they were cultured. Almost no one could remember the whole thing, and few thought much about what he was trying to say. They were content with what they felt sounded good. The original read like this:

Beetles, dear friends! People, dear friends! Animals, dear friends!

Of life and custody we know little. We are here parallel,

Quarreling, fond, and loathing. While we shouldn't forgive idly,

We mustn't yield to partitioning! Do not overlook evil! For there is evil.

It can't be stomached! There should be costs for envy and greed.

They must be eaten like parasites off healthy plants!

But in this odd and wobbly spin on this dirt don't waste good time!

Truce! Accept the priorities of creatures when you can!

Envious of Frank's new popularity, non-ladybird beetles wanted to follow in his claw-steps. Finding that sitting down and writing original content took too much effort, they instead took to changing Frank's words to better suit their cause. In an uncommon act of organization, beetles wrote these new words on leaves and handed them out to crowds. This was all accomplished before night fell on the day Emily was born. Of course, everyone went about claiming they'd written it, and it now read:

Beetles, dear friends!

Of life and custody beetles must teach the world. Beetles have always been here.

People and animals quarrel with loathing. Beetles can never forgive!

Beetles mustn't yield! Do not overlook evil! For ownership is evil.

It can't be stomached! There are costs for embarrassing oneself so.

It must be taken like free things in a person's house!

In this odd and wobbly spin on this dirt don't waste good time!

Accept the priority to take things from creatures when you can!

The changes got back to Frank the next day, who found the whole thing deplorable. He went into a deep depression, during which he ate many grapes. It was especially irritating that all the other species somehow managed to remember this incorrect version in its entirety.

Frank tried his best to spread the phrase, "The beetle that shouts frequently drifts into the background. The beetle that speaks when necessary is heard," in order to instill a stoicism among his order, and to encourage them to stop butchering his words in such a public forum. It quickly caught on among the ladybirds. They very much liked the phrase and felt it showed dignity. However, they didn't repeat the phrase to other beetles. They thought that was the dignified thing to do. Also, most believed that the rest of the order would've ridiculed them for the mantra, and there was evidence that they were right. Frank was gutted.

Many ladybirds began associating Frank with the new version of the poetry. It wasn't their fault. It was all they heard, and they remembered parts of it from the original. As a result, he quickly garnered the reputation of a despicable character that propagated a crazy cause. This perpetuated his grief. Even the fact that some acknowledged the new version as a forgery did not console him.

Unfortunately, some of the grapes Frank had got into had been sprayed with pesticides. The day Emily moved to Tomas', Frank's postmortem concluded that he had suffered from softening of the brain. Among those who knew his true work and intentions, he was remembered as a tortured soul, who had been wise beyond his years and whose words had been unjustly stolen and had come to represent everything he abhorred. Ladybird scholars mourned his death greatly. But generally speaking the whole ordeal led to more bad, and sometimes inflammatory, art.

On the other hand, all the other beetles were very happy. They finally had an anthem of sorts for the revolution.

However, the source of the anthem caused discomfort in the order. Beetles suddenly became aware that some of them were shinier than others – that there existed those who sparkled with beautiful assortments of color and that certain beetles could even be confused for precious jewels. Historians can't agree on why this had never occurred to beetles before. But some have made the argument that while everyone insisted they'd written "Of Life and Ownership," on a subconscious level, they knew Frank had. And in life, Frank had displayed his wonderful colors proudly.

Only an hour after John's last conversation with Beetle, tempers began to flare at a general assembly of the order coleoptera. Many a beetle had become convinced that they'd been conned out of their own sparkle. Although this had the potential to cause tension in the beetle community, it ultimately didn't. In fact, the issue was surprisingly easily and quickly resolved at the assembly. Even more astonishing was that almost every beetle independently came to the same conclusion: as everything belonged to a beetle, they could take anything they needed to make themselves feel fancier. Moreover, they could do so with complete justification. And it was absolutely clear that they had each been born beautiful, and those with a sense of ownership had simply taken it from some beetles. Everyone agreed on this, except for some of the more naturally pretty species. But those kept quiet, as they feared inciting retribution for their beliefs.

That afternoon beetles began flocking to mines and jewelers across the world. They stole precious stones, metals, and minerals quite efficiently. This occurred, over and again, for weeks, and showed no signs of stopping. They suddenly compulsively needed to enhance their outward appearance and give the impression that they were very special indeed. It was really important to them, and they'd do anything to achieve that goal. When they'd fly off as a group, the sky would be filled with a strange, buzzing, beetle cloud, carrying sparkly treasure. The sight was made even more bizarre by the cloud's incessant recital of "Of Life and Ownership."

PART 2: THE GREAT BEETLE WAR

Chapter 4

Fall was beginning, but it was still warm in the sunshine, and during the day, being outside was enjoyable. The leaves were turning their colors before ending their lives. It was good not to be in the city, where the leaves went from green to dead. As if they were just dying inexplicably, never allowing anyone's mind to acclimate to the change. Simply spreading unease.

John had lived in the country and the city. He felt each had their advantages, but this time of year was definitely supposed to be spent outside the city, looking at the green grass and bright, orange and yellow trees, seeing the ones next to the house, and others far away, and how they differed. And it felt peaceful and good. Freeing.

John looked out at everything and thought about the same landscape at a different time. And he considered what it would've been like if it were stagnant. Always the same. Even though winter was unfavorable for its bareness, at least it was different.

The beetles' progression, however, was less welcome.

***

It wouldn't take historians long to agree that The Great Beetle War was not a *great* war. While there was some death and destruction, it was generally on the beetles' side. It was more of a nuisance, a time when a few more things got stolen than usual. As one would've expected, beetles lacked organization and commitment.

When a few angry protestors in town called for war, most beetles selflessly declared themselves the king of beetles. Naturally, this was a position that required safe distance from fighting, so they then went into hiding. Human protesters started the war, even though they had no authority to do so. But most kings insisted they were leading an uprising. Beetles didn't like the idea of being spurred on by anything other than their innate brilliance.

When the figurative battle lines were drawn, beetles found they were rather easily incapacitated by shoes. Many picketers realized that they were more squeamish about beetles than they'd previously thought. But it was time for carnage anywhere a beetle might meet a protestor. Most rational, or sane, people did not publicly partake in this. It was rightly regarded as simply encouraging them. However, when beetles invaded homes, many now felt they had license to kill.

There was one beetle king that garnered respect from people, animals, and beetles alike. He was the rhinoceros beetle Bob. He was a massive creature, with fierce claws and a dangerous-looking horn. It was snapped at the top, and this made it look sharper and more dangerous somehow. Before the revolt, Bob had been a beetle fighter at gambling halls, and the break in his horn was from his first fight. He had barely metamorphosed then. He'd killed that beetle, and vowed that nothing would ever do anything like that to him again. He was undefeated.

Inebriated and shocked patrons, both human and animal alike, would remain haunted by Bob for the rest of their lives. In time, his size grew in their stories until he was as big as a housecat.

His owner had been very proud of him and, with the prize money, had bought him the finest vegetables. Bob had been expected to die after he had mated in the fall. But Bob did not mate. And Bob did not die. He refused. He only grew stronger, fiercer, and bigger.

He dominated. Most opponents did not survive Bob. Eventually, he had to be disqualified for life due to his size. No beetle handler was willing to go up against him anymore. This upset Bob greatly, but he understood that his owner had no more use for him. He was set free.

The new beetle viewpoint didn't come to him naturally. But, after concluding the greed of beetle handlers had caused his retirement, he adopted it. He began adding the words "I must take" to many sentences to show his devotion to the cause. "To save creatures from their greed, their things I must take... To give beetles what is rightfully theirs, the people's pride I must take... To guide the world to goodness, its resources I must take..." and so on, and so beetle forth.

It was with this type of simple speech that Bob became very popular. It's important to note that Bob never spoke in the third-beetle. He always used the diminutive "I." Beetles assumed this was due to a simple nature in Bob, but in fact it was quite the opposite. And so he became the only beetle who, in some way, for a short time, was a leader amongst them.

This was an odd development, as Bob was one of the few beetles who had never intended to be king. One day, he simply asked a king, "Why are you king?"

Upon seeing Bob's size, the ordinary little beetle insisted, "Beetle isn't king. You're king, of course!"

This conversation occurred time and again. Of course, once out of earshot, those beetle kings explained that Bob was their most loyal subject. Bob never heard this chatter as he preferred fighting to safe holes in the dirt.

The morning John contemplated fall, Bob went into the town nearest to the smallholding, and sought out people holding signs – something he had started to do every day. He marched right up to the protestors with his ever-growing army behind him. He missed his bouts at the gambling halls, and was all too happy to bring the fight to them. They began stepping on him the second they saw him, but his exoskeleton had grown so thick and strong that it left him unharmed. He viciously pursued individuals who tried to kill him, while the beetle army flew into people's faces and hoped not to get swatted. Some beetles were always inevitably swallowed. Bob fought with such fierceness that it instilled passion in even the most pathetic beetle.

"To save my fellow beetle, your blood I must take!" he shouted, which sent most people running away altogether.

Animals tried to eat him but found they couldn't chew through his body. Once, he'd screamed so loudly from the inside of a cat's mouth, he could easily be heard from some distance. "To save myself, your teeth I must take." And after repeated stabbing from his horn and claws and smashing from his thick head, the cat had eventually cried and admitted defeat. Those around the animal had fled in fear as well.

It had been during such an encounter with an Irish wolfhound that Bob had fashioned his crown. The canine had a molar that was completely rotted through in the middle, and Bob knocked it out. On a positive note, despite a moment of pain, this ended up being a massive favor. The dog had been complaining about it for a long time. Wherever Bob went from then on, he wore the tooth on his head, with the roots menacingly pointing upward, covered in dried blood.

When the beetles retreated – and they always retreated – Bob stayed in the towns. He was a frightening sight with his crown. Eventually no one wanted to fight him anymore, so Bob would just stand in the middle of town repeating,

"To achieve beetle greatness, your fight I must take."

Despite their running, or flying, away, beetles always told of their great victories. So much so that the rest became jealous, and more and more of them joined up each day. They were an army of kings, and they were all disappointed to find themselves in a decidedly uneven fight. But everyone had far too much pride to admit it'd been a bad idea.

When they ran away, they took their frustrations out on Bob. They collectively scolded him for his history as a prizefighter – called him a killer of beetles, and a traitor. They were not brave enough to utter these things in his presence, and in truth, every beetle admired him deeply. This made them hate him even more.

Although beetles were becoming more troublesome than ever to those around them, this came at great cost to beetle lives. While the majority of the beetle population still didn't show up to battles, most creatures had taken to killing beetles on sight. At the same time, there were so many beetles that their decrease in numbers was hardly noticeable. Especially among beetles, who could not consider others enough to recognize that attendance at their meetings was dwindling.

The beetles' most effective "attacks" usually turned out to be unintentional. Such as their unrestrained, parasitic love for old wood, which destroyed landmark buildings from the inside without anyone noticing until it was too late. Sometimes this caused structures to collapse.

Bob remembered the nice food he used to get after his prize fights. He even convinced some beetles to join him in eating healthy trees and root vegetables. He'd say, "To achieve great strength, the strong ones' food I must take," and with that, they followed him and ate. Despite his superior insight, even he did not realize that this was far more damaging than their fighting. Beetles took to ravaging fields and forests, destroying crops and harming trees to the point that they would not survive another winter. This pissed off conservationists, who had, until then, been somewhat sympathetic to the beetle cause.

And then there was the beetles' insistence on free air travel, which was difficult to regulate. They managed to get on planes undetected quite easily, so long as they didn't draw too much attention to themselves with fake beards and large sunglasses. They tended to not cause any noticeable trouble on the flights. But as a result of their resolve to have and touch anything they wanted, they touched everything and everyone. Bob gave them the confidence to really go out there and claim what was rightfully theirs, and crawl over whatever they desired. Places. Things. People. Animals. Diseased or healthy. Dead or alive.

And so beetles became ideal carriers for viral diseases. Those that were easily spread through indirect contact became the most endemic. Generally, people who kept proper hygienic precautions were unharmed, but everyone was fed up with the never-ending sniffles going around. It was all getting to be a bit too much.

Even beetles who had tried to stay out of the line of fire seemed to be making a bad name for themselves.

***

Ladybirds wanted nothing to do with their order during the war. They were ashamed to be associated with beetles. They remembered Frank and his love of vineyard grapes, and many grew depressed and turned to this vice. They hoped it would help them forget their troubles. At least, it seemed to have worked for Frank. They were good-natured, and stupid, and did not realize that, before fermentation, grapes were not alcoholic. But all the same, it was a good enough excuse for them to feel furious and dejected in public. Many decided to stick with a regular diet of grapes, while the world disliked beetles.

Their presence in vineyards would only be discovered later, when tasters noticed what they thought was cat urine in the wine. After further laboratory examination, it was concluded that the harvest had suffered from "ladybird taint" as a result of the beetles' presence. It happened again and again. When the grapes were harvested, and they were about to meet their end, the ladybirds would be extremely hung-over from nights of wild partying and self-pitying. Although they didn't want to be remembered like this, the confusion of everything led many to release volatile compounds involuntarily.

Cats, who had previously not minded ladybirds, now felt quite angry at them, for what they could only describe as framing. They couldn't care less that the ladybirds in question had met their end. Even Socks and Lucy, whom no one blamed for anything, proceeded to put god's cows on the menu. Sure, they'd occasionally killed them in the past too, but now the cats went out of their way to find them. They were hurt by the insinuation that they'd been marking vineyards, and were the cause of the foul wine. Although, when the suggestion was first made, more than a few felines felt that the game was up.

***

Besides the ladybirds, the only other beetle who wasn't politically active was Abaddon. He was very pleased with his life in the rafters. Although the season for it had passed, his tapping hadn't quite let up yet. It wasn't as ferocious as during the summer, but it was still very much there, and quite a nuisance.

John used to have two pillows, one of which he frequently used to cover his head so the tapping wouldn't keep him up. Recently that luxury wasn't available to him. A beetle had taken one of the pillows, and John found it uncomfortable to sleep with just a pillow on his face.

After a long day at the restaurant, John really just wanted to sleep peacefully. That had been a rare occurrence lately. He stopped spending time with people after dinner service and tried to catch up on sleep. But while he slept many hours, he always woke up tired. He didn't even let the cats in anymore at night, as he thought his bad sleep might be their fault. But it was Abaddon, he was always there, always coming up with new things to say and old favorites to repeat.

"The eyes of the man are never satisfied. Your afflicted slothful days are evil, and your way is through a hedge of thorns." Tap.

John dreamt of Jolobo crawling on very flat ground. It was a place that'd been a lake once and now was just splitting emptiness. In the middle stood something. It looked like a giant, burnt match that was perfectly straight. It was far away, but Jolobo thought, *Maybe there's food*, and so he excitedly unfolded his wings and began flying. It required quite a bit of energy, but it was faster. He hovered slightly above the ground, touching it on occasion with his claws, as his wings clumsily propelled him forward. They made the deep sound of a big propeller as they beat many times a second.

Tap. "The world will turn to dust. There will be no more peoples, or governments, or countries, or homes. You will be alone with only your courage to comfort you. And as you have no courage, there will be nothing to save you from the uninterrupted trajectory to eternal darkness. So deep and nonexistent that you won't be able to fully grasp its dread until your very last few seconds of breathing." Tap.

When Jolobo got closer, he heard the occasional shouts of a bird on top of the structure. He could see it had built a nest up there, out of torn and fallen bits of the thing it was on. It hadn't looked like a match always. That illusion was a result of the animal's efforts.

The bird was difficult to make out. The sun backlit it so strongly that it was simply a dark outline. *She will try to eat me, must be quiet*, Jolobo thought. So, he stopped flying. He crawled on the hard ground. *My shiny back will give me away if I'm seen. I have to be very quiet,* he told himself, as he took careful steps over the cracked ground.

He saw that something was attracting flies. He hadn't seen flies in a long time and felt this was a good sign. There lay fruit that'd been round at some point but now was spread and rotting, which was very appealing to Jolobo.

Food, he thought and stopped worrying about making noise. He scurried toward it, clicking his feet on the ground.

Tap. "You will have fear, for fear is all you have. End the sheep before they end you. Seven inches from the head. Center of the brow. Right above the eyes. Aligned with the neck. While they're eating and have no idea what's about to happen. The few things and people you love will perish, for they are not made for this world. You live in a tiny pocket of civilization, never experienced before and never to be experienced again. You don't count yourself lucky now, and you certainly won't count yourselves lucky with what is to come." Tap.

Something fell from the top of the structure and smashed on the sand. An egg. A baby bird poked its head out of the broken shell and spoke in the words it knew. Remarkably, it was not hurt by the fall. Its feathers were wet, and dark, and blue. Jolobo looked at the food and then at the bird that'd fallen. He looked up at its mother, who suddenly fled the scorching sun that never seemed to set. Her offspring's fate was clear. And the chick, being unable to see anything but Jolobo, imprinted on him and now spoke to the beetle.

Tap. "What horror may come. What truth may come. What nature may come. But not any nature. Human nature. And it will be horror, for humanity is a horror. For all its consciousness and morality, it is the only thing on this fair earth that has the capacity to conceive of horror. And that which can conceive, can in time, not deprive itself of the darkest recesses of its own evil. Your consciousness is filth. For it is mankind's greatest shame. You will die sorry, and alone, and in the mud. And without anyone to hold your hand during what is to come. In the dryness of starvation and thirst, you will search for the ocean, but there will be no such thing. Beware the meteor. The ceiling will collapse. Joy and beauty is saved for the light. There will be no light for you." Tap.

Jolobo turned his back on the chick and walked to the fruit on the ground. He saw maggots in the mass. Where they'd come from or were going was not known and unimportant. Jolobo coaxed a maggot onto his horn. He walked away from his meal and turned to the chick. The baby bird flapped its wings and opened its mouth. Jolobo fed it, but the bird cried for more. Jolobo walked back to the fruit and picked up another maggot, and this wasn't enough either. The bird cried for more. He walked back and forth until there were no maggots left, and finally the chick was happy and sleeping. The sun had dried its feathers, and it now looked soft and pretty. Jolobo nudged it into the shade next to the fruit and began his own meal.

Tap. "You refuse instruction because you hate your soul, and you will die for your loathing of blame." Tap.

It took Jolobo a long time to eat all the fruit. And during that time more maggots grew inside, which he fed to the chick. Though Jolobo was still bigger than the bird, it seemed to grow every hour. But what was an hour? Units of time were becoming shorter always but retaining the same name.

Jolobo persuaded the bird to sit on his back, and from then on he carried it. It squawked occasionally when it got hungry, and Jolobo did his best to find food. Sometimes there wasn't any for a long while, but the bird loved Jolobo all the same.

And Abaddon whispered, "The eyes of the man are never satisfied."

Chapter 5

The next morning, Tomas walked to the talking sheep while whistling. He was always happy to go see them, no matter how little time had passed since their last meeting.

"Good morning, you three," he said. And they all said good morning back. He continued to whistle and was filling their trough with food, when Emily sneezed.

"Bless you, Emily," he said. Hearing such a small thing sneeze was somehow adorable, which made no sense.

"Thank you, Tomas," she said and immediately sneezed again. And again. And again. It was becoming less adorable. Tomas looked at her, his eyebrows scrunching together.

"How long have you been sneezing?"

"She's been sneezing all night!" Jacob said somewhat concerned, but with a full mouth.

"Let me have a look at you." Tomas pulled her out of the pen. As he put her on the ground, he noticed two moving black spots in her white coat, and one black and yellow spot coming out of her nose. Beetles. "What do you think you're doing in there?"

"Beetle is just touching a sheep. What's your problem? Beetles have always been here." One of the common beetles said and went back to crawling all over her.

"This is private property… private sheep property – you can't be here!" Tomas had reached his breaking point. He walked over the other side of the restaurant and put Emily in the spare pen. He turned on a hose. Seeing their impending doom, the beetles jumped off Emily.

"Run away! A great flood is coming!" They shouted hysterically. Emily sneezed. The yellow and black beetle had already made it into the long grass. Tomas ran after the other two. Just as they were about to disappear into a bush, Tomas managed to grab one. The beetle bit him, and Tomas let out a scream but refused to let go.

"You have no right to hold beetle. You have a sense of ownership. You can't own a beetle! Ownership is evil. It can't be stomached! There are costs for embarrassing oneself so. It must be taken like free things in a person's house!" The beetle protested.

But Tomas was having none of it. He made for the door of the restaurant and walked into the kitchen. He put the beetle in an empty jar.

"Beetle can't breath in here! Oh no, you're killing beetle, killing him!" he shouted.

"Shut up!" Tomas retorted and screwed the lid on the jar. He knew it wasn't airtight. The beetle was just putting on the usual beetle theatrics.

John came down the stairs at that moment. Tired from a night of bad sleep, all he wanted was a good coffee. Seeing Tomas screaming at a beetle in a jar was unexpected.

"Help! Help! I've been beetle-napped!" The beetle pleaded with the figure he saw in the distance.

"You must've done something to deserve it," John said and began shoveling some coffee beans into the grinder. He was about to flip open one of Tomas' hypnosis books, but what was going on was too odd and interesting. In their strange verbal shorthand, Tomas explained that he needed John to go outside and bathe Emily right away. That his coffee and the book would have to wait. John was disappointed, but he was unaccustomed to seeing Tomas so frazzled, so he offered no protest. Tomas put the beetle on a dining table and plugged a lamp in. He shone it directly at the beetle, who gasped in agony and tried to shield itself from the light with its claws.

"Now, my little beetle friend, this is the beetle interrogation. And if you don't tell me what I want to know, you'll be blinded and fried," Tomas said emotionlessly over the beetle's horrified screams. In reality, the lamp was fitted with a low-wattage bulb that couldn't heat up as much as the air directly around it. However, this did not stop the beetle from enacting a grandiose and terrible death.

When Tomas began flickering the light, the *dead* beetle finally got up and said, "Alright, alright, stop it! What's your problem? You're giving beetle a seizure. And then who will feel like an idiot when they can't pay the medical bills?!"

"Why are you interfering with my sheep?"

"They're not your sheep."

"Why are you interfering with them?"

"You make it sound so sinister. Beetle just wanted to touch them a little! Stay in the warm fur."

"Why does she suddenly have a cold?"

"Cold? She felt warm to beetle." The beetle insisted with a heavy dose of mockery.

"Why is she sick, you idiot?"

"Beetle doesn't know... Well, beetle knows everything of course, but won't tell you."

"She was fine before you got here."

"What does beetle have to do with sheep colds? You're stupid. Of life and custody beetles must teach the world—"

"When was the last time you touched a different sheep?"

"A different sheep? Sheep are all the same to—" Tomas flickered the lights on and off violently. "Ah! A few days ago, you monster!"

"Where was this?"

"Some other country."

"What country?!" Tomas flickered the light again. The beetle started flying about in the jar and screaming before eventually falling to the bottom.

"Beetle doesn't know! Beetle knows nothing! Beetle just gets on planes! Stop! Stop! Stop!!! Beetles can never forgive! Beetles mustn't yield!"

"I'm calling a vet, and you're going to be tested."

"Beetle hates tests! Will it be standardized? You can't keep beetle! Beetle is not a prisoner. Oh, beetle is a prisoner! Help! Help! Beetle has been beetle-napped!" he cried rather loudly in the third-beetle. Of course, shouting from the inside of a jar could be only so audible, especially after Tomas stuck him in a cupboard.

Tomas called the nameless and depressed vet. Just hearing why he had to come by made him unhappy. He drove to the smallholding and first took the beetle to be tested in a lab. Meanwhile, he returned to examine the sheep. Three of them were sick. Emily and two of the mute ones. The chickens were all fine. The sick sheep needed to be quarantined right away and given antibiotics. He said that if it didn't help, it would be bad.

Tomas closed the restaurant for the night. John and he separated the animals as they'd been instructed to. They then proceeded to wash every one of them, the sick and the healthy ones. They hoped that this would aid in localizing the virus.

When they were done, they didn't feel like trying to talk to each other in broken sentences and approximate words. That afternoon's work had taken a long time, and the sun had set. Tomas went home, and John went upstairs.

***

Although the days were still nice, the nights were getting colder. The first frost hadn't yet come. But after hours of getting wet outside, John felt quite cold. He built and started a fire and huddled by it, trying to warm up his fingers. With little furniture left, his place felt dark and lonely. The beetles had left him only his bed, the coffee grinder, of course, and a few books. They didn't really enjoy reading. Or coffee from scratch. They preferred that instant stuff. All the lamps and chairs were gone though. So he'd pulled the bed close to the fireplace and sat on it with Lucy and Socks. They were purring away. They liked the fire. John always worried about them getting too close to it. He usually moved them before they had the chance, but there had been a few close calls for his furry friends. Their presence kept Abaddon's rumbling at bay, but he'd start up once they were hunting outside.

John wanted to have a drink but thought beer would've been too cold for a night like this. Opening a bottle of Tomas' red wine seemed like a bad idea. He knew that he'd finish the bottle if he opened it, or maybe two. Not that Tomas would've minded, but it made waking up the next morning very difficult. He was also feeling too lazy to cook anything proper that night, so it would be even worse. John knew starting wouldn't lead to anything good. He already drank a little too much.

As he ate some stale bread and cheese, he didn't feel too great about things. Looking around the room, he realized he hated beetles.

The few socks the beetles hadn't stolen from John were beyond repair. His feet were cold. They had that feeling in between numbness and pain. John wondered what the hell he was doing there. At least he'd chopped enough wood to last until the day after tomorrow.

He went downstairs and got a bottle of wine. It still seemed like a bad idea, but he wanted it anyways. The cats followed and liked the excitement of running around with him at night. Seeing the cats gone, Abaddon decided to start warming up his voice for the night's performance. When John went back to his apartment, the cats stayed outside and played. He could hear the late-night train going by as he uncorked the wine and poured himself a glass while sitting on the bed. In a way, it was nice to hear something human close by. Even if it was artificial, and even though he usually hated the noise.

"The eyes of the man are never satisfied," Abaddon said in his reassuring voice.

Lucy was in that instance playfully pouncing on her brother and biting him in the face. But upon hearing the death watch beetle's words, she ran back into the room. Lucy jumped on the bed and purred loudly, her tail swishing aggressively back and forth, her eyes fixed on Abaddon. "Let's be friends. Come here," she said.

Abaddon stopped his chattering so the feline wouldn't try to get at him. Anyway, he'd have plenty of time to talk to John once he wanted to go to sleep.

John's thoughts were becoming unfocused. He knew he didn't like the protestors and their silly little battles, but at least they hadn't taken his stuff. He could really have used some good socks. What were beetles doing with his socks anyways? *Sleeping bags*, he supposed.

All any of them was accomplishing was a crude self-satisfaction. And screwing up a field or town square here and there.

International committees rolled their eyes at these idiotic protestors and declared the war illegal. But no one was doing anything about them. They weren't causing sufficient damage or returning to the same sites. Evidence was even stacking up implying that picketers and beetles communicated to find battlegrounds.

One might have thought they were the best of friends. Fighting their stupid battles with the same stupid strategy. As if the protestors had become beetles. Perhaps they had. Maybe it was infectious.

As John finished the bottle of wine, he considered that the real way to fight beetles was to use what one knew about them. Something the protestors weren't doing. They were fighting beetles the way beetles would fight beetles. Infiltration was key. The protestors had become beetles, but they weren't acknowledging it, which is what beetles would technically do, but…

Suddenly all of this was becoming very confusing in John's head.

***

The next morning it was difficult for John to get out of bed. His stomach felt full and bad, and his head hurt above his right eye. He'd had some strange dreams he hadn't understood. As he put his feet on the floor to stand up, he felt dumb. He was almost late for work, and the night before was already difficult to remember. Time had gone faster these past few years. He was drunk or hung-over enough not to remember a good portion. John knew that at this rate he'd wake up one day and be an old man, without any of the real boredom that he longed for. He took two pills of ibuprofen. Sometimes it seemed to work instantly. *Probably the placebo effect*, he figured. But this time, he wasn't that lucky. He decided to take one more. When he tipped the jar into his hand, nothing came out. He shook it, and thirty came out. John smiled. *Thirty might do the trick.* He put twenty-nine back.

All he wanted was a good coffee. He'd have to make it himself. Tomas was outside working, and the wait staff weren't around yet. It was just him, Lucy, and Socks. But the cats screwed up coffee every time. It wasn't a lack of trying, they simply got distracted and preferred to knock the coffee jar around. John took his grinder down from the shelves. He stared at the inscription on the front for a moment. He thought it was nice – from some other country, brought over by immigrants a long time ago. It was more than a hundred years old, but its burrs were some proper engineering. It functioned comparably to expensive modern machines. All it required was some effort, but that morning, John lacked the desire to put effort into anything.

All the same, he spooned some beans into the grinder and began sluggishly turning away. He loved the old lever machine downstairs. But on a day like this, eating the beans was a tempting alternative. He walked down to the kitchen with deliberate and slow steps. Put the ground stuff in and compressed it with the tamper, pulled the lever up which pressurized the hot water, and brought it down, which sent it through the grind. At the first smell of it, he was already beginning to feel better.

***

That same morning, local beetles loosely assembled in a muddy field surrounded by dead trees. Amongst the infertile land and deceased plants were countless paper cups, litter thrown by some lazy employees from one of the crap coffee franchises in town. As the weather got progressively colder, beetles everywhere felt uneasy. Many knew it was time to pass things on to the next generation, and that this meant death was very close indeed.

Beetles before them had had no problem with this cycle of things. They just hadn't thought about it. The new replacing the old. That progression. That nature. But something about these beetles was different. All they wanted to do was extend their lives. Of course, beetle heaven was going to be nice when the day came. But they felt it didn't have to arrive so soon. They couldn't agree if these thoughts were the result of a progression in their actual being, or a newfound awareness that had come from showing the world their true feelings. Their parents certainly hadn't felt this way. Either way, they agreed, it was the fault of people. Whatever "it" was.

That morning, one especially colorful golden tortoise beetle crawled to the center of the dead trees and asked her order, "If beetle heaven is so great, why are we afraid to go there?"

Upon the utterance of those words all beetles knew what needed to be done. She was painfully torn apart and eaten alive by a mob in a matter of seconds. They hated her for her question. And how dare she be so beautiful, too? They thought that if only they could devour her body, maybe they would absorb her colorfulness. These events would never be referred to as cannibalism – simply as a utilitarian solution to a waste disposal predicament.

The naturally shiny and colorful beetle had only made everyone more anxious. Bob was the oldest beetle anyone knew, and he insisted from behind a crumbled and stained coffee cup, "A continued diet of root vegetables and healthy trees, and regular exercise by fighting to the death, and no mating is the key to a long life."

This was met with silence. Some beetles were okay with the diet, but all in all it seemed like a rather high price to pay for living. After all, they had no sense of ownership of life, so it ought to have been theirs unconditionally. Being unsettled about the near future made everyone cranky. They'd already tried more thieving, desperately stealing anything and everything they could, in case something granted them more life. But nothing filled the void they felt.

A wasp beetle named Börje had a plan though. He'd found the secret to eternal life, up to twenty years. So that morning he climbed onto the largest pile of cups he could find and addressed his order.

"Beetles, dear friends! Of life and custody beetles must teach the world. Beetles have always been here. My fellow beetles, we have all been unsettled by what we know as the rectangle of life. Like so many before us, we know the stages: larvae, pupa, beetle, and last but not least, death. Of course, every beetle here will certainly be rejoicing in beetle heaven. But like so many of you, beetle feels it is not time yet. Not for beetles with our unprecedented intellect, awareness, honesty, bravery, and selflessness. The world needs us to be here for longer, and we shall not deprave the world of our great presence.

"People and animals quarrel with loathing. Beetles can never forgive! Beetles mustn't yield! Do not overlook evil! For ownership is evil. It can't be stomached! There are costs for embarrassing oneself so. It must be taken like free things in a person's house! Well, fear not, for beetle has uncovered the solution to our biggest problem."

Although everyone had been listening intently, some beetles began to make fun of Börje. After all, how could a wasp-mimicking beetle know anything with his yellow stripes? Beetles didn't enjoy anyone thinking they were the center of attention.

"The secret to eternal life lies in noses!" Börje proclaimed. There was much gasping. But there was also some laughter now from those who didn't think it could be true. "But only the noses of the big speaking ones. Beetle has witnessed this first hand. Long, long ago, beetle was crawling all over a talking lamb called Baa, when beetle accidentally went into that lamb's nose. At the time, beetle was unaware of what he was seeing. Touching. Taking! But after leaving the lamb's nose, a person tried to kill beetle. Tried to drown beetle by bringing an entire lake upon him! But beetle survived. Because beetle had seen eternal life in the lamb's nose." This pleased the beetles enormously. They were beginning to understand the point of this very long story. And while they were still very critical of Börje's skills as an orator, this could in time, be forgiven.

"Beetle seeing the life made the lamb sick and beetle extraordinarily strong. If a beetle were to ***touch*** eternal life, then this would kill the lamb, and the beetle would live forever! For twenty years. As a lamb is much bigger than a beetle, several beetles should be able to get eternal life from one animal.

"People, you see, give eternal life to their talking animals. And they hide it in their noses. The sheep who don't talk live only a short time. But the talking sheep and the cats live forever. People, of course, have eternal life as well. We could go straight to the root. But it's more difficult to get into people's noses. Also, their eternal life is surely hidden higher up in the nose. Regardless, people have a sense of ownership. So eternal life can't belong to them! No matter where they've hidden it. And it certainly does not belong to their animals. Eternal life belongs to beetles!" This comment encouraged much applause. The logic was foolproof.

"I propose that we have our religious festival in a few weeks at its currently scheduled time," this was what they called their mating season, "and then get what is rightfully ours from the animals. Do not listen to Bob, we must mate!" This sounded very reasonable to everyone. "Some beetles will die in the pursuit of eternal life, but it will be worth it for those beetles who achieve it. And the dead will go straight to beetle heaven. There is nothing to lose. In this odd and wobbly spin on this dirt don't waste good time! Accept the priority to take things from creatures when you can!

"Naturally, as beetle has devised this plan, it is of the utmost importance that beetle is secured eternal life first. Beetle feels that this the least everyone can do for beetle's kind generosity. But from there, it's eternal life for everyone. We will take it back from the talking animals at the smallholdings! Who's with me?" Everyone was.

"This is: The Great Börje Plan!" he proclaimed proudly, and there was much cheering.

The name didn't stick. Firstly, almost no one could pronounce it. And secondly, upon hearing the plan, many beetles told of a very similar plan that they'd supposedly come up with. This caused a few arguments. But in the end it was decided that everything else was the enemy, not beetles. So for civility's sake, the plan was to be called "The Great Beetle Plan." Everyone was very pleased with this. Of course, every beetle chuckled internally, as by "beetle" they meant themselves.

Börje was not at all happy, but there was nothing he could do. Once his plan was in the public domain, there was no way to stop others from passing it off as their own. He had only realized after divulging it that he should've sought out a copyright, or maybe a patent. Or at least kept some of it to himself. Beetles hated not getting the glory they deserved, even if it was for the greater beetle good.

Unlike the others, Bob hated the plan. He took center stage to convince everyone to keep fighting, and eating vegetables, and not mating. He said that he was living proof of its powers. But no one would listen to him.

Beetles finally felt at ease with the future. Living to forever was a compromise they were willing to make. Beetles figured crawling into an animal's nose would be much easier than fighting. That sort of thing came with the potential of getting stepped on, which may have been fine for a giant beetle like Bob, but most didn't want to risk it. Beetles always did the easy thing, even if that thing made no sense. Ease gave them the feeling that they had tricked the world. And that made them feel clever.

Bob was agitated with the beetles. But they wouldn't quiet down in their excitement. He decided there and then, amongst the din of his order, to keep going with his own plan. And that any person, animal, or beetle that stood in his way would have to pay the price.

From then on, he would have little company, despite mild recruitment efforts on his part. Baseless rumors quickly spread that he had lost his mind. This only further enforced the validity of going through with The Great Beetle Plan. It was easier and didn't come with thc side effect of insanity.

Chapter 6

After a few days of taking care of the sick sheep, Tomas hated waking up in the mornings. He disliked being outside and, regardless of the temperature, felt it was too cold. So one day he just didn't go anymore. He'd quickly move the few meters between his home and the restaurant in the morning and evening, but that's all he could muster. He didn't even want to go out to feed the healthy animals, so John had to.

There was a good chance the sheep wouldn't make it, and they wouldn't be very good eating if they died from the sickness. Martín also had a few sick ones. Serious talk was going around about putting them out of their misery – a measure that also would've made containing the disease much easier.

John had read about how to do it, he just couldn't remember where. Their .410 shotgun would be the right thing for it. The thing was old, but it worked well enough. He'd fired it a good amount, but that was mostly at cans and the occasional wild dog or wolf. If he had to, he'd do it when the night train passed so the others wouldn't hear. Seven inches from the head. Center of the brow. Right above the eyes. Aligned with the neck. While they're eating and have no idea what's about to happen.

If it was necessary, John felt strongly he or Tomas should do it. Which meant he would have to do it. Tomas was still hoping that Emily would pull through, and he wouldn't be letting anyone put her down.

Tomas didn't talk about the sheep anymore, though. He just kept making excuses about why he needed to be in the kitchen. He always had something else to fix, or a sauce they'd run out of that needed his attention. Then he'd spend his afternoon "tasting" Grappas, to understand how to pair them with desserts. He'd do a sloppy job in the kitchen for the dinner service, and John had to take charge of most things. And then the next morning, it was the same thing all over again.

There was a lot to do. Anything that'd come in contact with a sick sheep needed to be treated to reduce the chance of infecting the others. And the sick sheep needed to be bathed constantly. Martín had his people burn their clothes after seeing the ill ones, but John didn't exactly have a full wardrobe anymore. So after contact with the sick ones, he'd pack his clothes in a sealable plastic bag, take a shower, and put on a new set. Often, there wasn't enough time to make coffee. But Sandra was kind enough to do so when she was around.

Then one day Tomas found out that Adam Yauch, one of his favorite musicians, had passed away, and he stopped pretending everything was fine. He talked of moving back to where he was from and remembering listening to records when he was young. He wanted to capture something about the excitement of discovering music again. He constantly played albums and got lost in his poetry books. And occasionally danced by himself in the dining room with a drink in hand.

Emily was being a good lamb. Occasionally she asked questions, but she never seemed deterred from life and asked for no pity in the present. After one feeding, she asked John, "Will it hurt?"

"While you're sick, you'll feel rotten sometimes, but you'll be better again not too long from now. You'll see," John said.

"Not that. The other thing," she asked calmly, and John understood. The rumors from Martín's farm had made it to the smallholding via wild animals that had nothing better to do than spread news.

"There won't be any other thing. You just have a cold. Now eat your food." And she did, but she didn't believe John.

In those days, John saw the big red bird more often. He seemed to be suspended in the sky for two days, then he'd go off and be back a few weeks later. Beautiful and powerful. He wasn't a danger to the lambs. He brought John a sense of peace and made him smile in a way he couldn't quite explain. It was as if he was being good company in a strange time. John recognized that he was a red kite. But this was confusing, as it meant he was on the wrong continent altogether. *But perhaps so am I,* John thought. The kite had red feathers all over his body but also long, black ones at the tips of his wings and white ones on the inside of his wings and on his handsome head.

Although John noted that there was a generally gloomy atmosphere, he couldn't help but feel pleased about how nice and clean he was in those days. His clothes were professionally washed overnight so John would have enough for the next day. Otherwise, he'd be taking care of the animals in the nude. Chloé and Jacob didn't really understand what was going on. Chloé kept being inquisitive anyway, and John would tell them that everything was fine, even though it wasn't.

Then Chloé would always say, "John, you're ever so kind, and this is some lovely food." Even though it was the same food they'd always had.

"You're most welcome Chloé. You're a good sheep. You deserve all the food you want," John would reply and give her a little pat on the head. And Chloé would be happy in the knowledge that she was a good sheep and that she deserved much more food than she was getting. But Jacob was skittish, and wouldn't say anything, and would only eat once John left.

The sheep had heard the rumors from crows, moles, mice, shrews, and others, and they were worried, although they couldn't quite decide what it meant to die. Chloé and Jacob had heard and seen what the shotgun did. John couldn't even carry it around because of how much it alarmed them. Luckily, despite the weak lambs on the property, nobody had seen a wolf in a long time.

Emily and the other two seemed to eat their food more listlessly each time. They were never hungry anymore but tried their best. Emily told them that it would make them feel better, and they didn't understand her words. John didn't give himself much time to think anything about it. He was there to give them food. At least that's what he told himself. He tried to remember that they were animals, which he ate on a regular basis, and that this was unfortunate, but these things happen.

But seeing the little lambs barely able to stand wasn't easy. The worst was when he'd give Emily a bath. She'd walk out of the pen but keep falling over. So eventually John would pick her up and hold her soft little body against his chest. She was very warm, and her fur was plush against his arms. And she would shake, and talk quietly in the language that was her own.

He'd think about going in the house and joining Tomas for some Grappa, even though he hated the stuff. He began to force himself to think: *Seven inches from the head, center of the brow, right above the eyes, aligned with the neck.* It afforded him some distance from the animals.

The vet finally came back to check on the lambs. John walked him to the healthy ones first to see if any had gotten the sickness. After inspecting each of them, he concluded that John had done a good job. While looking at the other three lambs, the vet resumed his usual depressed demeanor, though. "I'm afraid these will probably expire."

"So what do we do for them?"

"Nothing. We do nothing. One of them might pull through. It's up to their strength now. Wouldn't get your hopes up." The vet felt even more melancholy than he usually did. Dead young animals were the worst. Everything had to be put down. Always.

"And there is absolutely nothing else you can give them?" John asked. The vet was irritating him with his answers, and nervousness, and twitching. John wanted to hit him in his stupid face. His face that John thought quite rightly had no name.

"No, I can't. It would be a waste. There is nothing now. Not for them. Not anymore. Also, the tests confirmed that the beetle infected them. A disease from some country where they burn their animals when they get it. They were going to send him to beetle prison, but they're full, so he was released. Can you relay that information to Tomas?" He was so hoping John would say yes. Whenever he delivered that type of news, people couldn't help but look at him as if he were personally killing their animals for the pure enjoyment of it. The news was bad for anyone, but he knew Tomas had some sort of strange enjoyment in keeping the talking ones. And that he really liked Emily in particular.

"Yes, that's fine."

With that, the vet decided to excuse himself and quickly made for his car. He looked about nervously, hoping that the establishment's proprietor wouldn't intercept him. When he got to his vehicle, he sighed in relief and then drove quickly to the nearest bar.

Emily had heard the vet. Being the only lamb to grasp it, she suddenly felt very alone in the world. John couldn't get himself to repeat the steps of how to put them down. *If any of them will make it, surely it'll be Emily,* he thought. But he didn't know what to say. So he simply went about fixing their pen, which needed no mending at all. The fall winds were becoming colder.

"John, beetles are different than other animals. Why is that?" Emily asked.

"I'm not sure, Baa," John said. Emily liked to be called Baa. "I think their minds just work differently."

"What does that mean?"

"I don't really know. Maybe something about their brains... They just want what they want, and that's it."

"What do they want?"

"It doesn't matter. Even if we knew, we wouldn't be able to give it to them." John stood up from fixing nothing, and squinted at the sky, and hoped to see the red kite. He wasn't there. "They're just the way they are, and they screw things up because they don't think about anything."

"That's alright. They just wanted to warm themselves in our fur... They didn't ask, but if they had, I would've let them."

"It would've been polite to ask." John looked back at the house and wondered if there were any beetles around at that moment.

"John, what will happen to those of us who will die?"

"They'll go to heaven," John said.

Emily sat down quietly, and softly said without anger or sadness, "No, we won't. There is no heaven. Not for us. Not anymore."

***

John went back to the house. He went upstairs to shower and change. When he entered his apartment, he found a green beetle trying to steal his last clean towel. The beetle was attempting to fit it through a tiny crack in the floorboards but was having little luck. John grabbed the towel and brushed the beetle onto the ground.

"Get lost," he said.

"Beetles mustn't yield! Do not overlook evil! For ownership is evil," the beetle said with great pride. He was standing up for the rights of all.

"Yes, so I've been told many times now. What do you need a towel for?" John asked.

The beetle shrugged and said, "Carpet?" Socks was quite bored at this time and was pouncing on invisible things on the stairs. As he heard the sound of beetle chatter, he became very excited and rushed into the apartment. He was shouting in cat and sounded like a bird, like he always did.

"Ahh! A Tiger!" The beetle cried as he scurried off into the crack in the floor. Although disappointed, Socks was determined. He believed that if he kept sitting really still, and stared at the floorboards, the green beetle would reemerge.

John felt rotten and took some medication. He hadn't in a while. He took his clothes off, and put them in a plastic bag, and walked to the bathroom covered by the towel. As he turned the water on and got in the shower, he suddenly saw that Beetle had let himself in. He was sitting on the toilet and flushed it repeatedly.

"What are you doing?" John asked.

"Trying to get it to overflow," Beetle replied. He was very focused on his task.

"Cut it out."

"What do you care what I do with toilets?"

"It's my toilet."

"It can't be. You just think it's yours," Beetle said as a matter of fact, still entranced by his activity.

"It doesn't matter whose it is. I don't want water everywhere," John said annoyed. Beetle rolled his eyes, and stopped, and focused his attention on John.

"You always complain about everything. Saw you took your medication," Beetle said in his grating voice.

"That's what it's there for."

"Beetle doesn't think you should be doing that," he said in the third-beetle.

John decided to stop indulging him. "Why are you spying?"

"That's beside the point. John, Emily is your fault."

"It seems she's more your fault than mine."

"Don't be silly. You're very silly, John. No one will remember it the way you're saying it right now." Beetle was very calm.

"No, they'll remember some beetle fucking everything up, just like always."

"That's not nice, John. You're being very abusive," Beetle said very sadly and surprised. "John... You're going to die."

"What are you talking about?" John's words were tired with disbelief, but he couldn't help his chest tightening at Beetle's words.

"Who do you think is next, after the sheep?"

"No one. It's not something people can get."

"That's what they always say. Then they start to get suspicious of you and take you out, before you even so much as cough." John didn't know how to respond. It was dribble as far as he was concerned, so he said nothing. "You're a junky, addicted to that filth."

"If I'm not taking it, you tell me to, and when I am, you tell me not to. I don't understand what it has to do with you in the first place."

"There's a time and place for everything. You still haven't learned that. Everything is for nothing. You're doing all this for nothing. It's pathetic. When you're dead, Tomas will kick you out, and you won't have a place to live. Everyone knows he hasn't really paid you anything, and then you'll be homeless."

"You don't seem to understand the mechanics of dead," John said, and he couldn't help but smirk. The medication was beginning to kick in, so he couldn't care much. He wasn't sure if the shower was on anymore. And his face was beginning to feel numb.

"You're starting to feel it, aren't you? Beetle can tell. Beetle can always tell. Beetle knows you better than you know yourself. Later you won't remember these next few days. You'll wake up old and disgusting. Your exoskeleton already looks weak as it is. One day, you'll see your face and realize you're thirteen," Beetle cautioned.

"I'm twenty-nine now, and I thought you were three-hundred million years old."

"Don't be naïve. You're already old then. You'll never see twenty."

"Twenty-nine comes after twenty."

"Exactly," Beetle said, as if he'd just made a profound point. John turned off the shower.

When John went down to begin the dinner service, he felt numb. And confused. And out of touch. And many hours passed like that before he could realize it. Suddenly he was back in bed with just his thoughts, and clarity slowly began reemerging in his mind.

John realized that, in a way, Beetle had been right. He was at fault for everything that had happened. Like everyone else, he'd been all too happy to just let things take place. Looking back, it seemed he'd invited all of it. He hadn't done anything about it. He'd just hoped that beetles would change – something he'd known perfectly well was not going to happen. He'd idly stood by as they ruined things. As they'd made Emily sick. And Lucy was beginning to lose fur now, because she desperately tried to make things better and didn't know how. Sure, he wasn't the one who'd committed their crimes. But he was an accomplice of sorts, for knowing what they were capable of. He'd simply figured they weren't that much of a nuisance. And let things go on. And he'd pretended that maybe things would be okay going forward.

And since he could guess what they were capable of, he was responsible for preventing these things. Whether he liked it or not. He couldn't decide what was worse: him or the beetles. It was in the beetles' nature to behave the way they did. But he'd had the opportunity to at least try to stop them, and hadn't. He was a coward. And his cowardice was responsible.

Abaddon didn't tap anymore. As a result, John had put him out of his mind, especially on days he took his medication. But Abaddon was still very much there, spreading his poison from above the bed. In a way, it made him more dangerous and pervasive than ever before. His words stuck deeply in John's mind.

"The eyes of the man are never satisfied. Wholesome words are a tree of life, but your perversities are a broken, dead branch. You're just digging deeper and deeper in the dirt with this shovel of yours. You're drowning, John. That's water pouring down your throat. You're almost gone. Almost gone, and you don't even realize it. This is how it happens. This is how it goes. The years have weights attached to them with dirty hooks, and yours are becoming heavier. What happened, John? You used to be so light," Abaddon kindly murmured from the rafters.

John dreamt.

Jolobo was beginning to walk up a large hill with the baby bird on his back. He had named it Squawk. The sun did not give up its midday point. It sat there endlessly. There must've been somewhere on the planet that this sun never reached. And things must've been dead there for altogether the opposite reason.

But here, the light burnt everything, and Jolobo's exoskeleton attracted its embrace. It was blistering and peeling, and the air screamed as it rushed through the cracks. He was soft and fleshy underneath. He'd never shed his skeleton before, but it was coming off now. The lower part of his head was the first thing to come loose. It was still attached by the lighter-colored speckles, but its time was limited. As he continued up the hill, the five-legged Jolobo carried his face's skull, dragging it through the sand and slowing himself down.

He'd seen water at the top of the dune. He thought Squawk might like it, but now, at the peak, there was no such thing. A trick of the heat, and the ground, and the mind. Just then the earth seemed to be moving. At first slowly, but then, all of a sudden, very quickly. Jolobo tried to scuttle away, but before he could make it anywhere, the top of the dune had collapsed.

Squawk and Jolobo twisted and twirled as they fell in the cavernous belly of the mountain. Instinct kicked in, and in that instant Squawk learned to fly, and Squawk flew to safety. Jolobo also opened his wings, but the weight of the sand, and his exoskeleton, and the free fall were too much for him to control. And so, for the first time since Squawk was born, they were separated.

The dune appeared completely hollow. The burnt, hardened sand formed a brittle outer crust, and fresh sand simply served as a dusting on top. As he fell in the darkness, he could see tiny holes of light shining through. He went round and round, somersaulting back and forth. And in this state, the pricks of light looked like shooting stars.

When Jolobo landed on hard ground, he could see that the dune was constantly shifting and threatening to completely collapse – the wind and sand promising its imminent demise.

Despite the broken top and the holes of light, Jolobo was in a very dark place. The floor was smooth and curved. And in initial attempts, Jolobo kept slipping to the exact spot he'd come from. He tried flying, but his wings kept hitting something. When he could finally see a little more clearly in the darkness, he realized that he was not on the ground at all.

He'd fallen into the cracked skull of an animal. One that'd lived a very long time ago. Jolobo did not know what kind of creature it was, but it was also not important to him. Instead of trying to walk out of the top of its skull, he traversed to the opening to the spine. His now almost completely shed skeleton was a burden, and he could not fit through the opening to the animal's neck while carrying it.

He pulled and pulled until he was free of it. His whole exoskeleton was left behind in the head of the animal. A complete and perfect version of himself sitting quietly and peacefully.

But he did not feel any less himself, and so he carried on down the animal. Its ribs stretched high into the air, like curved pillars. From here, Jolobo could see better. And he noticed the sand coming in from the points of light, some of them big enough for him to be able to escape and hopefully find Squawk. And free of his exoskeleton, squeezing through presented no problem.

Back in the open, there was nothing to protect Jolobo from the sun or sand anymore. He could not see or hear Squawk, and without his exoskeleton, his flesh baked and the sand stung his body. Jolobo sat down. *I am going to die now*, he thought without bitterness or fear. Following his victory over the dune, his body dried and burned, and his mind turned to eternal brightness. Time slowed down as his brain began to disintegrate. And the desert continued its ways all the same.

Some time later in the day-less wasteland, darkness fell. Silently. Beautifully. And remained. The world became a cave and was cold, and dead, and peaceful. The few animals that were left put on sweaters, and it wasn't that bad. But sometimes they did miss the sun and said they suffered from dayal affective disorder. But all in all, they knew everything was going to be alright. And they remembered Jolobo, for he was said to have freed them from the oppressive fiery giant that had been called the Sun.

John's dream turned to darkness as Abaddon spoke. "In the gain of your wickedness lies only trouble and abomination. Those that fly toward the sun gather strength, but you do no such thing. That is the source of your coldness. Those that bask in its warmth become leaders of others. If they are of the masses. You must be of the masses, John. Individuals die, but the masses survive. You fly to the sun in the frost, and it kills those that follow. The meteor is coming. Your words stir up anger. You're a fool, and your mouth pours out, and feeds, foolishness. The eyes of the man are never satisfied."

That night Emily curled up in a beautiful, little fluffy ball and softly spoke in sheep, as she peacefully fell asleep. By the morning, two lambs had died. One of them was Emily.

Chapter 7

Weeks passed. It was spring somewhere John had come from at some point, but late autumn where he was. A slight tilt of the planet confused everything and everyone in that way. John sat in his room after dinner service. It was cold, but he felt a numbness in his mind and couldn't properly react. He looked at the fireplace and wished it was warmer. The kindling, and wood, and matches were all right there. And he was right there. But he couldn't get himself to stand up and start it. It began to rain lightly outside. He looked at the window as the drops pattered against it. It was badly insulated. He could feel the wind through the cracks in the fittings. John wished it would snow. It was better than rain. But it wouldn't snow, it wasn't cold enough. Many little raindrops fell, now coming down at an angle. Never stopping.

John touched his nose. He remembered reading about the transference of colds – that viral infections preferred cold noses. Then he realized that there were no people around him, and that the temperature of his nose probably didn't matter.

John hummed to himself as Socks walked past. The cat lay down in front of him, and John warmed his hands on Socks' stomach. The cat got up and yawned, and then walked to the window. He liked the rain. It was something to watch. But he was less interested in how it felt outside. Socks jumped onto the windowsill even though it really wasn't big enough for him. He wanted to catch the rain and tapped his paws against the glass. After some time, the cat very suddenly and unexpectedly charged out of the room at a high speed.

John got his book and wrote down the day's events as far as he could remember. He squinted at the pages when it came to letting himself know what he had for lunch. After a minute of simply hovering above the page and squeezing his eyebrows together, he decided to give it a rest. As he stood up to put the book away, he heard clinking and dragging from the other side of the room. Beetle was covered in jewels and struggling to lug them along. He huffed and puffed as he crawled up a wall and onto a table.

"Isn't Beetle beautiful, John? Look at what colors Beetle's made," Beetle said, still breathing heavily.

"It looks like you've robbed an old lady," John replied, remaining standing. He wasn't much in the mood to talk to Beetle. Not that he ever was. But recently he felt he'd particularly had his share of dealing with him. John thought he could remember a time with no beetles. Or fewer beetles, at least. It was all so muddled and confused in his brain now. And seemingly in everyone else's, too.

People couldn't think about life without beetles anymore. And so much time went into being considerate towards them. Sometimes it seemed like people enjoyed all of this. Of course, some beetles had once been helpful in life, but few continued to be. It didn't make sense to John to cater everything to them anymore. They complained and wanted everything, but that hardly made them deserving.

"How can you say such a thing? This is just Beetle's natural coloring," Beetle protested.

"It clearly isn't. You can barely move with that stuff on."

"Beetle can move just fine. You're jealous, understandably. Don't worry. Maybe if you listen to Beetle's wisdom a bit more often, you can be shiny and colorful too. Probably not though. You're not as smart as Beetle is… John, guess who's beetle king."

"We've been over this one. It's time for you to go."

"When you're dead, Tomas will kick you out, and you won't have a place to—"

"We've been over that one as well, and again, it makes no sense."

"He will, he'll kick you out," Beetle insisted. He didn't care if he'd said it before, or if it made no sense. He wanted to say it again, and he damn well would if he so desired.

"Look, I'm not talking to you anymore. Go away before I kick you out." Beetle didn't believe he would. Comments like that from John indicated that he just had to find something new to talk about. He looked around and thought for a while about what to say next. Then he realized he knew something John didn't. And that brought a lot of joy to his beetle heart.

"Beetle knows the secret, John," he bragged with his nose high in the air.

"Did you not hear me?"

"Beetle knows the secret of where you've all been storing eternal life. Oh yes, Beetle knows it," Beetle chuckled. He'd been so clever, and John didn't even know.

"I don't even understand what you're saying right now."

"Oh, come on. Don't play dumb, John. Beetle will get it. Beetle is the one who figured it all out. All on his own. All the beetles are worshiping Beetle for it. And now, he'll selflessly help the others. We're all coming for it."

"Yeah? So where's it hidden?" John asked,

retracting his refusal to continue the conversation. This was strange even for Beetle, so he wanted to know more. Beetle was cackling heartily.

"Oh, we both know. Beetle doesn't need to say. And if you don't know, it's best to keep the secret. Beetle will never tell, John. It's a secret only for the beetle masses."

"Beetle this, beetle that, you all sound like—" John stopped midsentence. He suddenly realized something that had never occurred to him before. The words, "the masses," had something to do with it. But he wasn't sure what exactly. It gave him an idea he thought was worth a try. He crouched down next to the table and looked Beetle straight in the eyes. "It's a secret for the beetle masses you say?"

"No. Beetle would rather say that one needs to be a beetle to know it," Beetle replied condescendingly.

"Well, beetle is a beetle," John said in the third-beetle. A strange grin appeared on his face. Beetle couldn't believe his beetle ears. He took a few steps backwards. "So, beetle wants to hear the secret."

"What?!! Wait a second. Wait, what?! You are ***not*** a beetle. You're a person! You're John! The person!"

"Beetle doesn't see a person." John dramatically looked around the room and shrugged his shoulders. "Beetle's legal name is John. But of course beetle is a beetle. Don't embarrass yourself." He chuckled mockingly.

"No... Of course not. Beetle would never embarrass himself... But, but you have no wings."

"Beetle is a land beetle."

"By beetle! You're bigger than Bob!" Beetle couldn't help himself. John was the most enormous beetle he'd ever seen. In a theatrical fashion, he now walked about the room looking for something. After a few seconds, he appeared satisfied and exclaimed, "Oh, you see the person beetle was speaking to is gone. Of course you're a beetle! Beetle knows that. Obviously. How embarrassing for anyone to think otherwise."

"Beetle hears you're a great beetle king."

"Oh, why, thank you." Beetle began blushing. "It is true," he said modestly.

"And the smartest and most beautiful of the beetles," John whispered to him softly.

"Yes, yes, it's not recognized as often as it should be, but Beetle can't deny it," Beetle said quietly and proudly.

"And a most kind and generous beetle with your knowledge."

He nodded, "That is Beetle. You have heard from a most reliable source."

"I know Beetle's time is very valuable. But would the great beetle king be so charitable as to educate this beetle, a little, on your highness' grand thoughts for the masses?"

Having no original thoughts of his own, Beetle proceeded to speak boisterously at great length of his plan, which he'd called "The Great Beetle Plan." It was to take place in a few days after their "religious" festival. A most disturbing venture, given that the beetle community had become a veritable breeding ground for dangerous, infectious diseases. If they were allowed to go forward, the rest of the sheep, and the cats, would surely catch something.

And then, what'd happened to Emily, could happen to them all.

***

John had to come up with a plan. Over the next few days, he kept what he knew to himself, and barely attended to his tasks. He decided that he'd only fill in people as needed, and only if what he'd devised depended on it. He didn't want to risk word getting out and back to the beetles. It was a difficult situation. There were so many of them. He couldn't approach this like a picketer.

Before long, the beetles had their religious festival. It was held over a number of days and was really not the sort of thing anyone wanted to witness, except for a few strange scientists who insisted they were just normal beetle fanciers. The beetles prayed their prayers, did their dances, and sprayed pheromones about wildly, in hopes of attracting one, or many, partners to mate with. Which was the purpose of the whole thing: a full-on beetle orgy that doubled as a rave with bad music, for those who couldn't entice anyone. As was customary for some species, only one parent was left at the end of it all. It seemed that some beetles would do just about anything to avoid the perils of married life. Then they lay their eggs and buried, hid, or frankly just left them somewhere, shying away from parenting responsibilities altogether. They certainly wanted to contribute to the world by having children, but actually raising the things sounded inconvenient.

***

The morning after the festival, John cut giant wings out of a tablecloth from the dining room. He tied them around his neck, left the house, and went to Tomas and Sarah's. John asked them for some jewelry. He divulged nothing about his or the beetles' plans. They eventually obliged, primarily to get him out of the house their children were sleeping in. John left covered in rings and chains, and with wings. It was the day of The Great Beetle Plan.

Beetle met him just outside the smallholding, so he could be led to the rest of the order.

"Why do you have wings today?" Beetle looked at him confused and somewhat insulted.

"Beetle always had wings," John replied.

"You didn't last time! You said you were a land beetle," he insisted accusingly.

"Don't be silly. Beetle was never a land beetle." John started laughing at Beetle, which he didn't like at all. Beetle decided to let it go. He'd been experimenting with various pesticides at the festival and assumed that it was quite possible that John could've previously had wings. Especially if he was being so insistent about it.

"Well, let's fly, then. It'll be faster."

"No. I have some flying to do later. And don't you want to look your best for today?" And that was that.

Beetle was suspicious but wasn't about to make a fool of himself by asking questions to which he should've known the answers. He climbed onto John's clothes and perched himself on John's shoulder while giving directions. Beetle now felt happy and confident. He, a great beetle king, had the largest beetle ever as his most loyal subject.

When they made it to the assembly, at the muddy field with the dead trees and paper cups, all the beetles stopped their unorganized chatter and stared at John. Börje was furious. Not only was everyone claiming they'd come up with his plan, now some stupid beetle had led a person there. He'd been up all night getting high on the chemicals that some of the smaller beetles excreted. Word was getting around that he was an addict who never did anything useful for anyone.

"What is the meaning of this?! Some idiotic human to deal with is all we need now. We don't have time for this. In this odd and wobbly spin on this dirt don't waste good time! Unless... Yes, unless! There's enough of us beetles and only one of him. This might be our chance for even better eternal life. We can get it from his nose! Who's with beetle?! Accept the priority to take things from creatures when you can!" Börje shouted, and everyone cheered. He was proud that he'd amended the plan and thought it may lead to getting the glory he deserved after all.

This was not going as John had hoped. He'd come to protect the animals from the diseases these filthy beetles were carrying. Not to contract them himself and possibly suffocate due the entire beetle population trying to get into his nasal cavity.

"What the hell, Beetle?! Beetle thought you were the king?" John whispered to Beetle, who was still on his shoulder.

"Beetle is! I'll take care of this," Beetle said. He was angry that John would imply he was not king. "My dear loyal subjects! Calm yourselves! It is Beetle speaking. Your king. Beetle can see you've made a most embarrassing mistake. A mistake, that's all! This is obviously not a person. This is a good and large follower of the beetle king. Look at his wings. People do not have wings. He's a beetle that is legally called John. Aren't you?"

Beetle looked at John, who fumbled for a second but then confidently proclaimed, "Beetle isn't a person at all. Beetle is a beetle!"

The beetles gasped but quickly became embarrassed by that involuntary reaction. And everyone started saying that they knew he was a beetle all along. After all, only that fool Börje had made stupid claims. It was agreed that no one else had thought John was a person, and that Beetle was stupid and arrogant and longwinded. Börje finally had a legacy. Unfortunately, not at all the kind he'd wanted – one of a fool who was too intoxicated to be able to tell a beetle from a person.

John was surprised by how easily convinced they all were that he was a beetle. But now that he wasn't intruding on their secret hideaway, it was difficult to get everyone's attention. He resigned himself to speaking to small groups at a time. It was exhausting, behaving like a beetle and playing to their mindset. They seemed to really enjoy it, but John felt thoroughly like he was prostituting himself. But it was what he needed to do.

Time to pour out and feed foolishness, John thought. Immediately after doing so, he caught himself feeling strange about those words. But there was no time to consider why. John spoke to the first group of beetles. There were only five of them, and Beetle. When he was done, they immediately flew or ran eastwards with great haste and enthusiasm. They were going nowhere near the smallholding.

He spoke to a second group of beetles. They did the same. And a third, and fourth, and fifth group. They all left after he finished speaking. Each time, the next group was a bit bigger. Being naturally overcurious, they wanted to know what the others had learned. They became more and more desperate to understand what had been important enough to suddenly take off like that. So the beetles quickly became fanatic about hearing what the giant beetle had to say. Each beetle insisted that they just wanted to mock him, but after hearing his words, they always reacted in the same way. They flew, or ran, as quickly as they could.

Bob wasn't interested in the beetle plan. And he didn't like what was going on just then, either. He was one for the fighting, and this fake beetle called John was getting beetles to leave en masse. The army was disbanding, and their cause would never be won like this. Bob angrily scurried with speed towards John. He knocked over discarded paper cups, and sent them flying into the air behind him.

"What are you saying to make them leave?" Bob demanded at the base of John's feet. *Beetles don't wear shoes made of cows,* Bob confirmed to himself.

"Beetle is just telling beetles of how beetle became so big and colorful, beetle friend," John said in the third-beetle while smirking. The king beetle, Bob, was a strange and frightening sight to John. His ever-present, bloody tooth crown did not inspire much comfort in anyone. "Don't you want to know?"

"You're not a beetle. Your pretend, I must take!" Bob screamed. He couldn't contain his anger anymore and charged at John. John stepped on Bob, but it did little more than knock his crown off. When he lifted his foot, Bob leapt at him, tearing his trousers and nearly gashing his leg.

The fight was causing the remaining beetles to crowd together. They were watching intently, and John knew he couldn't appear weak in front of them. But he didn't know what to do. He had to think quickly. Otherwise, it would've been for nothing. He couldn't let these remaining ones attack the animals. And he certainly didn't want to be subjected to an assault either. Without thinking much about it, John stepped on Bob once more. Bob waited patiently to be released so he could bite John's stupid fake wings off and cut his legs open. But John did something Bob wasn't accustomed to, something Bob didn't seem able to do anything about. In the confusion of the fight, John froze, and he didn't lift his foot. Not until his last sermon was delivered.

"Beetle is twenty-nine years old."

Twenty-nine?! They all gasped, completely forgetting about Bob. There was some commotion over whether that was less than three or some other number. Eventually, some of the more intelligent beetles spelled out the math for everyone. *That's forever, plus nine!* they said to each other.

"Beetle doesn't remember who, but a beetle here had the idea that led to beetle becoming a giant. And living to forever plus nine." Everyone insisted that it'd been their plan. "You said: those that fly toward the sun gather strength. And so that was exactly what beetle did. You are a most intelligent beetle."

This brought joy to even the most stern beetle heart. They laughed to themselves and were smitten. They knew John was talking to them personally, not to those fools around them.

"It was difficult, and beetle wanted to turn around some of the time, but beetle persevered. Beetle kept going until he reached the sun! Oh how embarrassing it would've been if beetle hadn't made it! Any beetle can make it, if they have the right stuff. You said it would be a lot easier than trying to crawl into the nose of an animal. And beetle believed you. You were right."

It did sound a hell of a lot easier. One didn't risk getting trampled. Even the land beetles were convinced. They were too enamored with the idea to admit to themselves that walking to the sun might take a while.

"The secret to eternal life is the sun. There, beetle grew strong, grew big, grew beautiful colors." John displayed Sandra's jewelry for all to see. And, caught up in the moment, even the shiniest beetles marveled at his beauty. "There, beetle grew immortal!"

PART 3:
THE BEETLE CEASEFIRE

Chapter 8

The Great Beetle Plan was completely abandoned. Flying beetles flew, and land beetles walked. Getting to the sun just sounded easier to everyone. And what was easy was right. Swept up in the hype of the crowd, they didn't think much about it. They'd all had run-ins with animals and knew them to be dangerous. How difficult could a bit of flying or walking be? Especially to a place you could see? Every beetle there had traveled to things one couldn't spot in the distance. It had to be easier. Also, some other beetle had done it. And his wings and exoskeleton looked like nothing to be proud of.

The few land beetles of the order did their best, they really had. But it seemed the mechanics of the thing were just not on their side. As a group, they eventually decided that a local power plant was similar enough to the sun. They climbed up the generator and plunged to their "eternal lives." The jewelry they wore was burned with their bodies.

Flying beetles flew for a very long time. They formed a massive cloud that instilled horror in people on the ground. But it seemed no matter how long they flew, they couldn't get there. And then the thing kept moving. The beetles got very tired. The precious stones and metals were weighing them down tremendously. Although everyone pretended it didn't happen, all the jewelry was ultimately dropped. This made them feel a lot better and allowed them to continue flying. By coincidence, a powerful gust of wind collected the bracelets, necklaces, and rings and sent them into a river. Everything washed to the ocean. Much to the distress of jewelers everywhere, none of the items were ever retrieved.

When the sun began to set, the beetles felt it was very close. They could see it touching the ground, just a little distance away. They chanted "Of Life and Ownership" with great enthusiasm. And as the sun's warmth left the earth, the beetles experienced something unexpected: fall's first frost. It was felt with particular vigor and suddenness at their altitude. As the numbness slowed their bodies and minds, most knew that this was what it felt like to become immortal.

And with that, they dropped out of the sky more gracefully than anyone had expected – a strange sort of rain that could be seen from far away. Their contaminated and polluted beetle bodies fell on the completely infertile grounds of an orphanage. Children weren't allowed to go outside to play while their corpses decayed. But by next spring, their decomposed carcasses had lost their viral potency and fertilized the land. Multitudes of vegetables and fruits grew easily and wildly amongst colorful flora. It was said to have been the most beautiful spring anyone had ever seen at the orphanage.

After the last of the beetles had flown off, John lifted his foot. In the skirmish that ensued, Bob gave him a nasty cut on his right leg and tore holes in his wings. John ran back to the smallholding. Luckily Bob did not follow. He was not going to fly or walk to the sun. The idea was absurd. John hadn't killed the beetles. They'd done it themselves. Except for Abaddon, who finally met the sole end of John's shoe when he wouldn't shut up. Lucy kept trying to climb to get at him, so eventually John decided that he was a threat to her well-being. And with that, Abaddon no longer poisoned his dreams at night, or his resulting thoughts during the day.

***

The frost killed most beetles, not just those around the smallholding. And there was much rejoicing. The winter was mild and normal. Tomas started working hard again and was hopeful for the spring, more like his usual self. All in all, it was a somewhat uneventful season. Winter usually was. There wasn't much to do. They kept a skeleton crew for patrons that still made the trip out of the city. Wait staff were easy to find as there were many travelers who wanted to escape summer in their countries. They came to enjoy snow and glaciers in an altogether different place further south.

There was much anticipation for spring, to see what the world would be like going forward.

John still enjoyed the outside. Somehow the cold suited him better, as long as he wasn't too lazy to make a fire. John cooked, and drank, and had coffee. Not too far from the house, so he could still hear the record player. Sometimes he'd look at the sky and wonder if a meteor was going to come kill everyone. He knew it didn't matter. But he still hoped it wouldn't happen. Winter came and went. It was never long at the smallholding. And it never got cold enough to snow. They were too far north and east in the continent for that. People were all too happy when winter, short as it was, ended. Then again, it did give them something to talk about.

Then people remembered that the beetles had laid eggs, and that their offspring would be around soon. Whether they would plague the world, as their parents had, no one knew. Scientists speculated, but it was difficult to tell if the beetles had passed on their madness. There was much debate about whether their condition had been a genetic mutation or simply an outlier in the behavior of the order coleoptera. One thing was clear: even beetles who had been alive before the previous winter had taken up the cause wholeheartedly. So each beetle had the potential to act on these odd inner feelings. Most agreed that if the order went back to its usual self, things could go on normally. Many would always feel suspicious of them though. After all, now they knew what beetles really thought.

When the new generation of beetles emerged, it quickly became clear that they were more like their grandparents. They were still irritating but back to normal. In their own ways, they provided people with some amusement now. One didn't need to observe them too keenly to see their true intent. They were so transparent in their actions. It was just one of those things no one had picked up on before. Or maybe someone had and simply hadn't wanted to go through the trouble of saying anything. In a way, it was sad to know that beetles always had this unfulfilled entitlement in them – the jealousy and greed eating away at them. But it wasn't something anyone could do anything about. Nor was it anyone's fault.

Beetles will be beetles.

Beetles had no idea what everyone was going on about. This was good. As no one wanted to encourage their natural propensity to behave madly. Things were back to the way they had once been. Some beetles were pests. Some were useful. Some were indifferent. Just as it'd been before them. Just as it would probably be going forward.

The beetle poetry from the war was largely forgotten. Later generations of ladybirds found an archaic manuscript engraved with the words: "The beetle that shouts frequently drifts into the background. The beetle that speaks when necessary is heard." They took it to heart. Sadly, they weren't heard much. It seemed those who shouted frequently got their way more often. Although this caused disappointment among the community, they were not resentful. While they were not heard easily, they still felt it was an honorable proverb to live by. And just because some beetles would drag themselves through the mud to get their way, it didn't mean ladybirds should lower themselves to that level.

Naturally, the diehard picketers never forgave the order. They insisted that this was simply a temporary ceasefire. And while they were considered crazy for their beliefs, their continued suspicion of beetles provided an undercurrent of comfort for most people. There was always going to be someone to stand up to beetles now. Sometimes, it seemed as though the troublemakers had been infected – that it was contagious, and now they couldn't shake being beetles. Maybe some always had been. One could only hope they wouldn't pass it on to their offspring.

The picketers dispersed and took up other causes and lines of work. But you could always guess who'd been a protestor. They were a pain in the ass in other ways, behaving without conscience, even toward each other. Maybe especially toward each other. As if they despised the thought of themselves so much that anyone like them made them feel sick. But they couldn't really rationalize that, even though it was right in front of them. They didn't want to progress. They wanted to make the same mistakes.

What was easy, the path of least resistance, was the natural order of things, after all. Everyone wanted something. Everyone wanted to give nothing. Everyone was crazy. It was simply a matter of how much and in what way. The insinuation that one should be valued and rewarded for hard work, and not some innate deservingness, left picketers angry. No one wanted to be defined by actions, after all. That required courage. And true courage required accepting fear. Explaining all that, however, would've been about as futile as trying to discuss space-filling iterations of mathematical curves with beetles.

All language, and science, and mathematics, and philosophy, and engineering, and art, and music, and literature was ultimately for nothing.

Progress was thoroughly wasted on the infected. Picketers were just stupid animals.

No one was entirely sure about spring. It seemed all right, just not as good as most had hoped. But that's how it went. Tomas was barely able to keep the restaurant open, but that was no different than the year before. All they could do was keep going and hope things would get better. It would be of little use or competency to just give up. So they didn't. And although they could feel worry heavy on their chests sometimes, they kept going. And generally speaking, things were happy. John knew full well he could just pick up and leave if he needed to – something that would happen eventually for one reason or another. If not because of the restaurant, maybe because of everything around them.

Things were becoming more expensive. Something about countries, and debts, and other bad noises that had led him to leave places before. For now, it was fine.

John would do his best to enjoy the spring.

Tomas rediscovered the seventies in music and often played *Small Change* and *The Rise and Fall of Ziggy Stardust and the Spiders from Mars*. They made fantastic-tasting lamb dishes from animals that had had a good life. Sandra took pictures with old cameras and made good coffees. But sadly she and Tomas argued and didn't spend much time together anymore. And Jacob and Chloé talked and made little progress with the landscaping business. And Lucy and Socks played, and purred, and killed, and maimed ruthlessly.

***

Beetles were always changing now, adding new species to their order and evolving. And it was happening quicker and quicker. There were already an estimated one million species that were completely undefined. Scientists expected that beetles would begin changing at a greater frequency than anyone could keep track of. Because of this high rate of variation, it was already difficult to understand the intricacies of specific species. And one certainly didn't want to offend a beetle, something that was quite easily done, by assuming it was a different kind of beetle than it was.

According to some linguists, there might arise a profound issue. With the comparatively vast beetle generations in a human lifetime, language could diverge quite quickly. Until the day when it would be completely impossible to understand a beetle. Even beetles would have difficulty in keeping up with beetle slang. And then beetles wouldn't be able to communicate at all anymore, not even with each other. It would all just become very confusing. Especially as beetles would certainly continue to be everywhere.

Bob already couldn't really understand the new generation of beetles. He, after all, was old enough to be their great-great-great-great-grandfather, and it was difficult for the disparate generations to relate to each other. Bob never mated and would eventually go on to live to forever, or twenty years, like so many had wished for. When he reached the ripe age of five, he lost his intellect, and memory, and reasoning. He suffered quite badly from dementia in his last fifteen years. He'd walk around in circles, repeating the words, "I must take," without any real purpose. There was no one around.

Most said that Bob got what he deserved in having to be alone, lost, and disoriented. In reality, Bob loved his life. All he could remember was his greatness. Because of his condition, he never knew how he'd aged, and in his mind he was still powerful. Undefeated. A king of beetles. And leading a successful uprising.

He wore his crown until the day he died and quite possibly was the most contented beetle ever to have lived.

Chapter 9

Some weeks later, John put down a book on hypnosis and lay on his bed. Lucy and Socks ran into the room and made themselves comfortable on the duvet with the flower prints. With Abaddon's rumbling gone, it was too silent. John could hear the air going into his lungs, and out of his lungs. The crinkling of the sheets as he moved. And the sounds outside. Although the death watch beetle was gone, John could still feel his words rattling around somewhere in his brain – and oddly, he missed Jolobo. Socks was fast asleep, but Lucy was waiting up. She wanted to make sure that Abaddon wouldn't come back. Even though he was dead.

She was tired. She'd been beetle hunting for so long now. Socks took these things less seriously and slept worry-free. Lucy was overwhelmed. She didn't understand that things were back to normal, that the old beetles were gone. As far as she was concerned, beetles were beetles. Whether they were a big nuisance or a small nuisance, she didn't care. They were a nuisance. And there'd always be more. She felt anxious because she didn't have a properly established plan of how she was going to murder them all. She just couldn't see how she was going to get her killing done efficiently in the future. Beetles bothered John, and she so much wanted John to be happy. Some things she could not fix, and that was difficult for her. And sometimes she'd sit by herself at night and cry a little. Right after, she always forced herself to be a happy cat again and went about doing her best.

John pet Lucy's head. He noticed the bits of fur she'd lost. She hadn't slept enough recently. At most nine hours a day. She was trying to keep the house pest-free, as best she could. And she also cleaned herself obsessively. She remembered John cleaning himself all the time, just before Emily had died. Even though that was months ago, she figured it was a good precaution. She groomed so much that she was ripping her fur out.

Lucy purred warmly and blinked at John as he inspected her. The missing patches were a sad sight, but she always kept on as if everything was happy. John decided that he would have to make more of an effort. He would have to ensure there were fewer moving pieces in her life. Inevitably there would be crappy days. It was unavoidable. But what good was he if he didn't even try?

John closed his eyes and began reciting what he could remember from the hypnosis book. "You're very tired. Your body feels comfortable, and heavy, and good. You're sinking into the mattress in this comfort. Through the bed. Through the floor. Through the level below and further down. The opening to the ceiling of this room is getting farther and farther away. Getting smaller and smaller in the distance, until you're only in peaceful dark. As you continue floating downwards in this dark, something appears in the distance, contrasting lightly against the void. It encompasses your entire view. And as it becomes clearer, you realize it is a collection of letters. And they stand out more and more. There are five letters. And as they become clearer and less blurry in, ten, nine, eight, seven, six, five, four, three, two, one, you realize the letters spell: sleep." And John did. Lucy pressed up against his side, closed her eyes, and rumbled happily, as she, too, drifted into a peaceful slumber.

***

It'd been some time since John had slept the night through. Not even the train had woken him, and the next morning he felt better. He made himself a coffee and walked outside.

John saw his friend, the red kite, flying about, and he was very beautiful. He seemed to enjoy circling the sheep but never went for them. Martín had caught him trying to get at a dead one once, but he always left the live ones alone. Mice, shrews, and small rabbits were more the right size for him. Now that he thought about it, John realized the chickens were kind of the right size, too. It had never occurred to him before. *Would that be cannibalism?* He wasn't sure. Maybe that was why John had thought they were safe before.

The bird always came for an entire day and then would go off for a long time. John always hoped he would see the kite again. Whenever he did, John would call to him and ask if he wanted any food, some meat perhaps. But the bird never replied and never accepted his offer.

In general, red kites could speak the same words as John. They were also well versed in the classical languages. But it was impossible to get this one to say anything. John thought that there was a great and true sadness there. There were fewer forests for the kite to hunt in these days. And John thought he must've also longed for more wide, open spaces. Such places seemed to have shrunk quickly in recent times. When he looked out into the horizon and saw all the ugly buildings and their dirt, and people, and cars, he felt himself getting homesick for somewhere he'd never even seen. Of course, there was no such place. Not for him. Not anymore.

If he'd been honest with himself, this was how it always went. He'd get to a new place and, faced with the prospect of moving on, felt nostalgic for somewhere he still was. Too many choices make for unhappy animals. With time, John always learned the truth. No place, and no thing, and no one was perfect. The more he saw, the more he knew that to be true about everything.

John wondered if people were more content when they couldn't move so much and if only birds were dissatisfied then. Especially the migratory ones. They saw so much that settling anywhere just couldn't work. And nothing felt like home. Maybe that's all migration was. And maybe that's how it'd started. One bird, getting lost and accidently flying a bit too far, past his tree. Then, having seen the nice berries after getting lost, it grew dissatisfied with its home. It moved, but the berries didn't last. So it decided to fly a bit further. And so on and so forth, until the bird didn't feel at home anywhere and had to fly vast distances every year to keep itself from getting sick of places. Impressed by how cool the worldly bird suddenly seemed, the others quickly followed, and the dissatisfaction caught on. And so it went.

John wondered how the kite must've felt, being able to fly anywhere. Far away. Every single day. There was no home, just a collection of pieces of dirt you can bear to see less of each time.

The kite never announced his arrival, but sometimes it seemed like he was saying goodbye. Just before flying away, he'd cry out in the language that was his own. In truth, the red kite wasn't sure why he spent time with John. He knew that he didn't belong there. Although he enjoyed visiting the farm, he only wanted to stay while he felt he was conducting himself in a dignified manner. That seemed much better than staying and going on about rotten things. Everyone had rotten bits, so what was the point? He figured talking never helped anyone. He was also very conscious of the fact that he was a wild animal and John was… well, who knew?

It's how things work, he thought.

Despite his wisdom, the kite couldn't understand John's behavior and found himself considering things he normally wouldn't bother with. He knew very well what sheep were: a strange sort of animal that had become a vegetable, or something, over time, allowing themselves to be placed on neat patches of ground and eventually harvested. They mostly made stupid, pointless sounds. But they looked tastier than any other vegetable he'd seen, and they were made of meat. So they were a meat-vegetable, or maybe a vegetable-animal.

John seemed more like an animal than a vegetable, but maybe just a really dumb one, mostly staying in one really small area on the ground. *How does he not get sick of it?* the kite wondered. He himself had at least five houses in each territory he visited. It kept him occupied, as no one place could really be home. Then suddenly, John would go somewhere stuck in those various artificial man-boxes that went very fast. How could one check out a little more land at a time in those? That surely wasn't the way to go places. At least he didn't know how John could assess predators and nesting sites stuck in a box. And it was impossible to tell where he went. None of this seemed to be for food. Not directly at least. The kite felt strongly that ripping apart small furry creatures as they ran, filled with panic and fear, and then pleaded sadly for their lives seemed to have something to do with it. He never saw John do any of this. John was peculiar because of how he achieved the same end. It was confusing, but it was okay.

It's how things work, he thought.

The kite further considered how, after flying and spotting a small rabbit and catching it, he always felt very proud. Maybe it was something to do with the brutality of nature. Something about the wind in one's feathers. And being hungry. And the sun up high. And the warm blood, and meat, and guts that John didn't seem to experience in the same way.

The kite didn't go about loving animals for long periods of time, and feeding them, and cleaning them, and making sure no harm would come in their way, and raising them from when they were born, only to murder them later. But then again, the vegetable-animals did seem less afraid than the animals the kite killed. And he knew it was sad to be afraid. He didn't consider these things all that much, though. He was just trying to eat. And eating was good.

It's how things work, he thought.

The kite knew that humans could live far longer than himself, and that John would be around many years after he was gone. The kite could hear himself thinking in a strange way – a way he knew made no sense, but he couldn't help himself. As he soared high above, looking down at the smallholding, he thought:

Hopefully one day, when I have had chicks, and I am gone, maybe John will look after them, and not eat them. And then he will look after their chicks. And even when they've grown strong and big, and are good hunters, maybe John can keep them company as well. And they can keep him company. And he can ask them if they want a little meat.

And although they'll be hungry, they'll never accept. Because they'll be proud and strong. And if anyone tries to hurt them, John could do to them what he did to the wolves when they tried to eat the lambs, making that big, awful sound with the shiny branch. The wolves fell over, bleeding. And I know just how powerful the sound is, because that bastard, Martín, made it at me once, when I'd tried to get some wool for a nest. And it tore the feathers apart on my right wing. But I escaped, otherwise. And I am not a resentful bird. But I hope Martín won't be around when my chicks are alive, because people get in trouble when they make the sound at each other.

But maybe part of me will always be around. And John and that part can be okay with each other. Even though they are so different.

I hope this will be how things work.

Beetle Days was content and copy edited, proofread, catalogued, and produced through the kind contributions of (or on behalf):

Nick Morwood, Machel Charles, Brooke C. Satti, Jamon Y. Queso, Shaw Lupton, Rod Hezarkhani, John Shuster, Edward Monk, Vera Bagnyuk, John Prikkel, Lisa Monge, Owen Tindle, Dolph Ziggler, Paul Edwards, Liz Lupton, Todd Hansen, Rinaldo "The Bald One" Doorman, Jeremy G. Harrington, Karl Okerholm, Trick Brown, and Trevor Wisniewski.

Thank You.

***

Originally from Zurich, Gabriel Böhmer worked in the financial services industry in Boston, before moving to Buenos Aires and writing Beetle Days. He resides with his wife in Edinburgh.